Wishing From Afar

고대하다 연연하다 성찰하다

한국대표시인54인선집
Collection of Korean Poems

Wishing From Afar

고대하다 연연하다 성찰하다

이소정 · 이덕원 옮김
Translated by
SOJUNG LEE · DUKWON LEE

이영희 그림
Illustrated by
YOUNGHEE LEE

맥스media

서문

90년대 들어 해외에 처음 나와 살 때, 현지 친구들이 한국은 어디에 있는 나라냐고 물어오던 시절이 있었습니다. 생각해 보면 당시에는 외국인으로서 인종차별도 받고 부당한 대우를 받기도 했었습니다. 25년이 지난 지금은 토론토 시내 중심가의 가장 큰 전광판에 한국 가수의 앨범 광고가 걸려 있고, 친구들은 한국 드라마와 방송을 저희보다 더 열정적으로 찾아보며 또 밤을 새웠다고 얘기합니다.

"우리나라가 세계에서 가장 아름다운 나라가 되기를 원한다. 오직 한없이 가지고 싶은 것은 높은 문화의 힘이다."라고 무려 백 년 전에 말씀하셨던 독립운동가 백범 김구 선생의 염원이 요즘 더욱 마음에 와닿고, 한국문화에 대한 세계적인 관심에 그저 감사할 따름입니다.

이런 트렌드에 힘입어 저희 부부는 문학을 사랑하는 세계인에게 한국인이 사랑하는 시를 영문으로 소개함으로써 언어 장벽에 가려져 있던 한국 시^K-Poems^를 선사하려 합니다.

우연한 계기로 한국 시를 번역하기 시작했습니다. 시가 주는 순간적이지만 깊은 울림과 언어의 섬세함에 빠져들어 언젠가부터 시를 적어 두는 노트를 지니고 다녔는데 이를 보신 아버님께서 번역을 권유하셨습니다. 다른 언어를 사용하는 사람들과도 한국 시가 주는 감동을 함께 나눌 수 있다면 얼마나 의미 있을까 하는 생각에 젖어 즐겁게 작업을 했습니다. 일주일에 한 편씩 영어로 번역하는 프로젝트를 2년 동안 진행하다 보니 어느덧 112편이 모였습니다.

한국 시는 격변의 한국 역사와 문화를 품고 있습니다. 식민지, 한국전쟁 등 어

preface

When we first moved abroad in the 1990s, most of friends that we met did not have any clue about Korea and often blankly asked where it was. Not unique to just us, we experienced racism and discrimination in our early days growing up as a minority. 25 years later, we now see massive billboard advertisements of Korean singers in downtown Toronto and have colleagues and friends who binge watch K-drama and shows more than we do.

For this reason, this famous quote by one of the most respected figures in Korean history 'Kim Gu' who fought for our nation's independence almost a century ago is particularly heartfelt nowadays. "My wish is that I want my nation Korea to be the most beautiful country in the world. The only thing that I desire infinitely is a power of a strong culture." We are grateful for the growing interest in the Korean culture around the world.

Building on this global trend, we would like to share Korean poetry that have been secluded largely because of the language barrier. We are thrilled to introduce Korean poems to the non-Korean speaking population and expose readers to diverse perspectives and styles. We have worked on a poem on a weekly basis and have compiled 112 poems over the past 2 years.

Korean poetry has a long history that meaningfully represents the country's culture and tradition. Korean poets sublimated our nation's complex emotions into literature. They expressed deeply rooted emotions

두운 상황을 이겨냈던 한국은 이를 문학으로 승화시켜 삶의 애환과 한[恨]을 담아내기도 했고, 때론 환희, 희망, 사랑 그리고 아름다움을 노래하며 시를 통해 상처 난 감정을 치유하기도 했습니다.

시라는 짧은 문학 안에는 시공간을 초월한 무한한 우주가 담겨 있습니다. 번역은 그 안에 담긴 한국을 전달하는 것이라 생각합니다. 시 고유의 분위기와 온도를 고스란히 지키기 위해 저희는 단순히 사전적 단어를 옮기는 것에 그치지 않고 시 안에 수놓아진 한국의 정서와 감성을 최대한 날것 그대로 옮기고자 부단히 노력했습니다. 단어 하나의 의미를 살리기 위해 사전과 씨름을 했고 때론 열띤 토론을 하며 수정에 수정을 거듭하면서 정교함을 더했습니다.

저희는 이 언어의 장벽을 낮추고 K-Poems만의 감성을 품은 우수한 작품들을 널리 알리어 K-콘텐츠의 폭을 넓히는 데 기여하고자 합니다. 또한 시를 중심으로 문학적 국제 교류가 활성화되고, 소중한 한국의 문학적 유산이 여러 세대에 걸쳐 소통될 수 있는 기회를 제공함으로써 선한 영향력을 끼칠 수 있길 바랍니다.

저희 부부의 번역본을 통해 세계인에게 K-Poems의 아름다운 결이 전해지길 바라는 마음입니다.

한국이 가득 담긴 시문학의 공간으로 즐거운 여행을 하시기 바랍니다.

이소정 이덕원 올림

2023. 새소리 가득한 봄날.

stemming from conflicts, invasion and war. They also exhibited joy, hope, love and beauty to convey meaning and to restore open wounds through poetry.

Every poem contains infinite interpretation in their lines. Translation is about delivering all of Korea found within each poem. We strived to preserve and convey that very sentiment and authenticity found in each poem and create a sense of connection to the past. Some days we had to dig deep to find the right word that we were seeking and underwent numerous revisions to finesse our work.

We wish that our translations break down that barrier, and lead to K-poems gaining greater recognition on a global scale. We hope that these inspire those who are unfamiliar with this genre and spread positive influence by generating opportunities for international cultural exchange over generations.

We would now like to invite you to the artistry and allure of K-Poems through our translation work.

Please enjoy your poetic journey through Korea!

With gratitude,
Sojung & Dukwon

1장 __ 고대하다 *To look forward to*

차례

2장__ 연연하다 *To dwell on*

3장___ 성찰하다 *To reflect on*

1장

고대하다

To look forward to

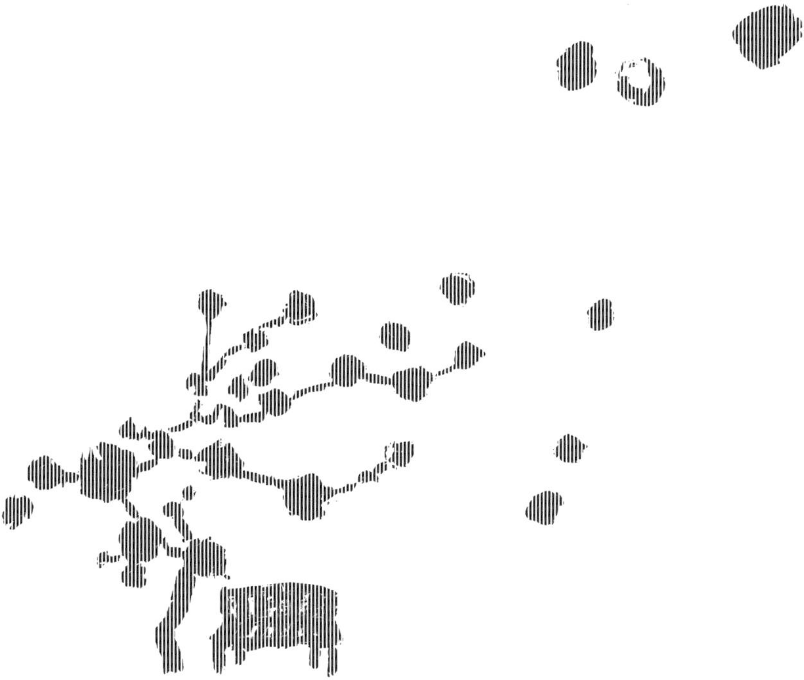

꽃 1
Flower 1

혼자서
Alone

그리움
Longing

사랑에 답함
Answer To Love

봄꽃
Spring Flower

봄밤
One Spring Night

3월의 바람
March Wind

초행
Path

봄날
Spring Day

달이 떴다고 전화를 주시다니요
Dear Me, You Gave Me A Call Because The Moon Rose

꽃
Flowers

경계
Boundary

풀꽃
Wildflower

혼자 생각
Thinking Alone

너에게 쓴다
Writing To You

뒤편
Rear Side

어느 봄날
One Spring Day

꽃 앞에서
In Front Of A Flower

인생미로
Beautiful Path Of Life

대추 한 알
One Date

내가 사랑하는 사람
Person That I Love

별똥별
Shooting Star

햇살에게
Dear Sunshine

산유화
Flowers In The Mountain

내 안에 머무는 그대
You Dwell In Me

벗에게
Dear Friend

꽃 1

다시 한 번만 사랑하고
다시 한 번만 죄를 짓고
다시 한 번만 용서를 받자

그래서 봄이다.

—
나태주

Flower 1

Let's love once again
Sin once again
Be pardoned once again

It's spring because so.

—
Tae-joo Na

혼자서

무리지어 피는 꽃보다
두 셋이서 피어 있는 꽃이
도란도란 더 의초로울 때 있다

두 셋이서 피어 있는 꽃보다
오직 혼자서 피어 있는 꽃이
더 당당하고 아름다울 때 있다

너 오늘 혼자 외롭게
꽃으로 서 있음을 너무
힘들어 하지 말아라.

—
나태주

Alone

Two or three flowers that bloom together
May be more harmonious than
Flowers that bloom in bunches

A flower standing alone
May be more confident and beautiful than
Two or three flowers that bloom together

Do not be disheartened about
Standing alone as a flower today
Feeling lonely.

—
Tae-joo Na

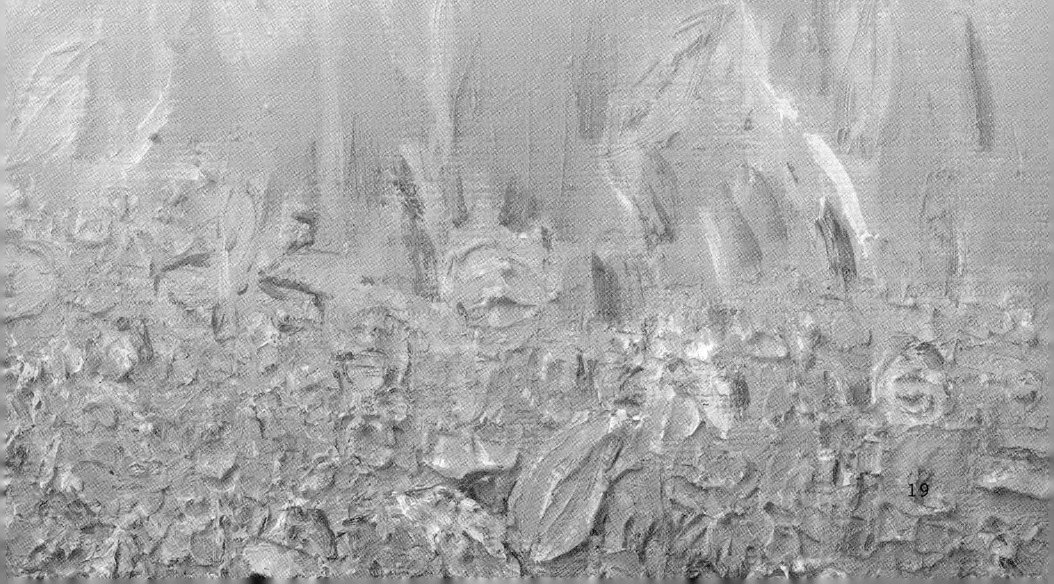

그리움

가지 말라는데 가고 싶은 길이 있다
만나지 말자면서 만나고 싶은 사람이 있다
하지 말라면 더욱 해보고 싶은 일이 있다

그것이 인생이고 그리움
바로 너다.

—
나태주

Longing

There is a path that you want to take when you're told not to
There is a person that you want to meet when you've chosen not to
There are things that you want to do even more when you're told not to

This is life longing
It's you.

—
Tae-joo Na

사랑에 답함

예쁘지 않은 것을 예쁘게
보아주는 것이 사랑이다

좋지 않은 것을 좋게
생각해주는 것이 사랑이다

싫은 것도 잘 참아주면서
처음만 그런 것이 아니라

나중까지 아주 나중까지
그렇게 하는 것이 사랑이다.

—
나태주

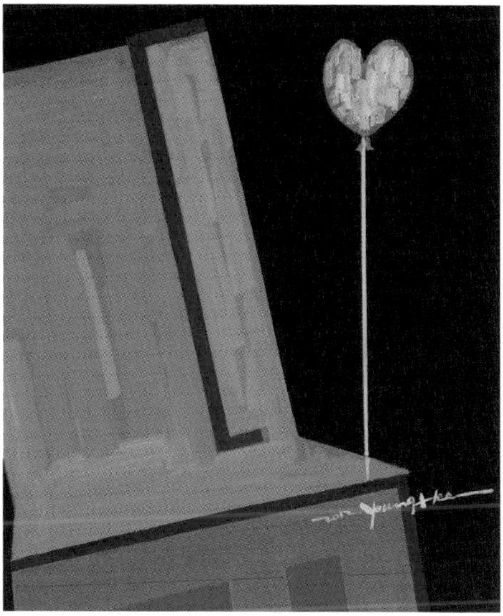

Answer To Love

Love is
Seeing unpretty things in a pretty way

Love is
Thinking of unpleasant things in a pleasant light

Tolerating what you dislike
Not just in the beginning

But doing so thereafter and forever after
That's love.

—
Tae-joo Na

봄꽃

꽃이 핀다
내 마음엔 너가 핀다
자그마한 꽃망울, 어여쁘다

봄날, 넌 나의 꽃이 되었다

너는 나의 봄꽃
너는 나의 설렘이다

순간의 스침에
이토록 오래 생각한다
한동안 오래 어여쁘다.

—
이경선

Spring Flower

Flower is blooming
You are blooming in my heart
Small blossom, it's lovely

On a spring day, you became my flower

You are my spring flower
You make my heart flutter

In a momentary brush
I dwell on thoughts of you for a long time
Interminably, it's lovely.

—
Lee Kyungsun

봄밤

이토록 아름다운 날에
이토록 어여쁜 너가 있으니
이토록 난 행복할 수 밖에

—
이경선

One Spring Night

On such a beautiful day
You are here beautifully
I can't help but be happy

—
Lee Kyungsun

3월의 바람

필까 말까
아직도 망설이는
꽃의 문을 열고 싶어
바람이 부네

열까 말까
망설이며
굳게 닫힌
내 마음의 문을 열고 싶어
바람이 부네

쌀쌀하고도
어여쁜 3월의 바람
바람과 함께
나도 다시 일어서야지
앞으로 나아가야지

—
이해인

March Wind

The wind blows
To open the petals of flowers
Still shy
To blossom or not to blossom

The wind blows
To open my firmly shut heart
Hesitant
To open or not to open

Cold
Yet lovely March wind
I, too,
Shall rise again with the wind
I shall go forth

—
Claudia Lee Hae-in

2018 YoungHee

초행

처음 아닌 길 어디 있던가

당신 만나러 가던
그날처럼.

—
고두현

Path

Is there any path that is not the first

Just like that day
When I went to see you.

—
Ko Doo-hyun

봄날

나 찾다가
텃밭에
흙 묻은 호미만 있거든
예쁜 여자랑 손잡고
섬진강 봄물을 따라
매화꽃 보러 간 줄 알그라.

—
김용택

Spring Day

If you just find a homi* covered in dirt
In the garden
While looking for me
Then just know I am off to view the apricot blossoms
Holding hands with a beautiful girl
Along the spring river of Seomjin.

—
Kim Yong Taek

* Homi: Korean gardening tool

달이 떴다고 전화를 주시다니요

달이 떴다고 전화를 주시다니요
이 밤 너무 신나고 근사해요
내 마음에도 생전 처음 보는
환한 달이 떠오르고
산 아래 작은 마을이 그려집니다
간절한 이 그리움들을
사무쳐오는 이 연정들을
달빛에 실어
당신께 보냅니다

세상에,
강변에 달빛이 곱다고
전화를 다 주시다니요
흐르는 물 어디쯤 눈부시게 부서지는 소리
문득 들려옵니다

—
김용택

Dear Me, You Gave Me A Call Because The Moon Rose

Dear me, you gave me a call because the moon rose
This night is amusing and wonderful
The brightest moon I've ever seen
Rises in my heart and I can picture
A small village at the foot of the mountain
I am sending you
My desperate longing
This aching heart
Along with the moonlight

Dear me,
You gave me a call
Because of the beautiful moonlight shimmering on the river
I hear the dazzling sound of scattering
Somewhere down on the flowing river

—
Kim Yong Taek

꽃

마음속에 박힌 못을 뽑아
그 자리에 꽃을 심는다
마음속에 박힌 말뚝을 뽑아
그 자리에 꽃을 심는다
꽃이 인간의 눈물이라면
인간은 그 얼마나 아름다운가
꽃이 인간의 꿈이라면
인간은 그 얼마나 아름다운가

—
정호승

Flowers

Remove a nail that is stuck in the heart
And plant a flower in that spot
Remove a post that is stuck in the heart
And plant a flower in that spot
If flowers were teardrops of people
How beautiful are the people
If flowers were dreams of people
How beautiful are the people

—
Jeong Ho-seung

경계

과거를 팔아 오늘을 살지 말 것
오늘이 미래를 잡아먹지 말 것
미래를 위해 오늘을 유보하지 말 것

—
박노해

Boundary

Do not live today by selling the past
Do not let the present consume the future
Do not put today on hold for the future

—
Park Nohae

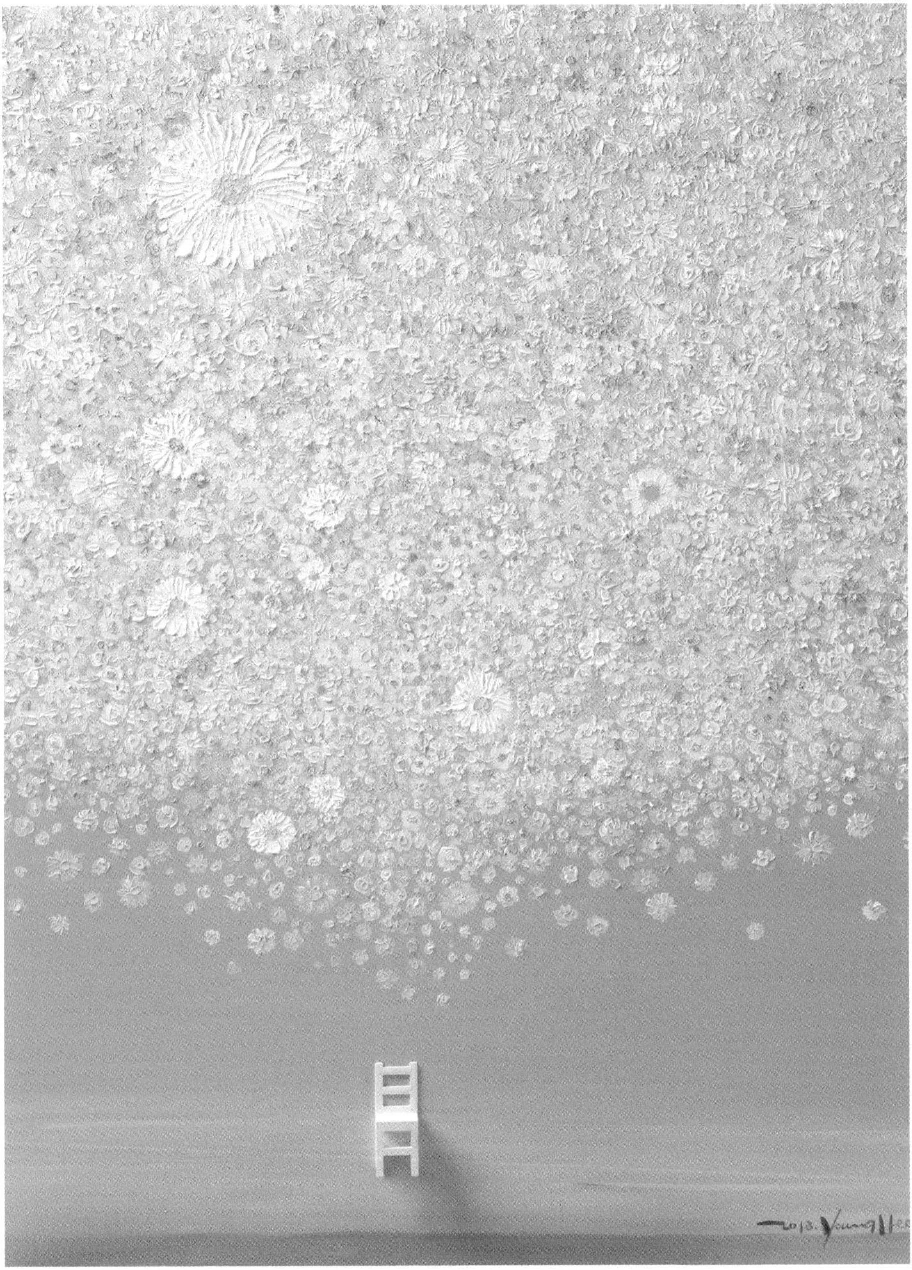

풀꽃

이름 참 좋다

언제나 싱싱하고
언제나 아름다운

넌
풀꽃처럼 수수해 좋고
꽃처럼 화사해 좋고

—
엄기원

Wildflower

It's a splendid name

Always fresh
Always beautiful

I like you
As you are pleasantly simple like a wildflower
As you are brightly radiant like a flower

—
Um Ki Won

혼자 생각

눈 뜨면 보이지 않던 그대가
눈 감으면 어느 사이에
내 곁에 와 있습니다

—
용혜원

Thinking Alone

Thou I couldn't see when I open my eyes
Stands right by me in a flash
When I close my eyes

—
Yong Hye-Won

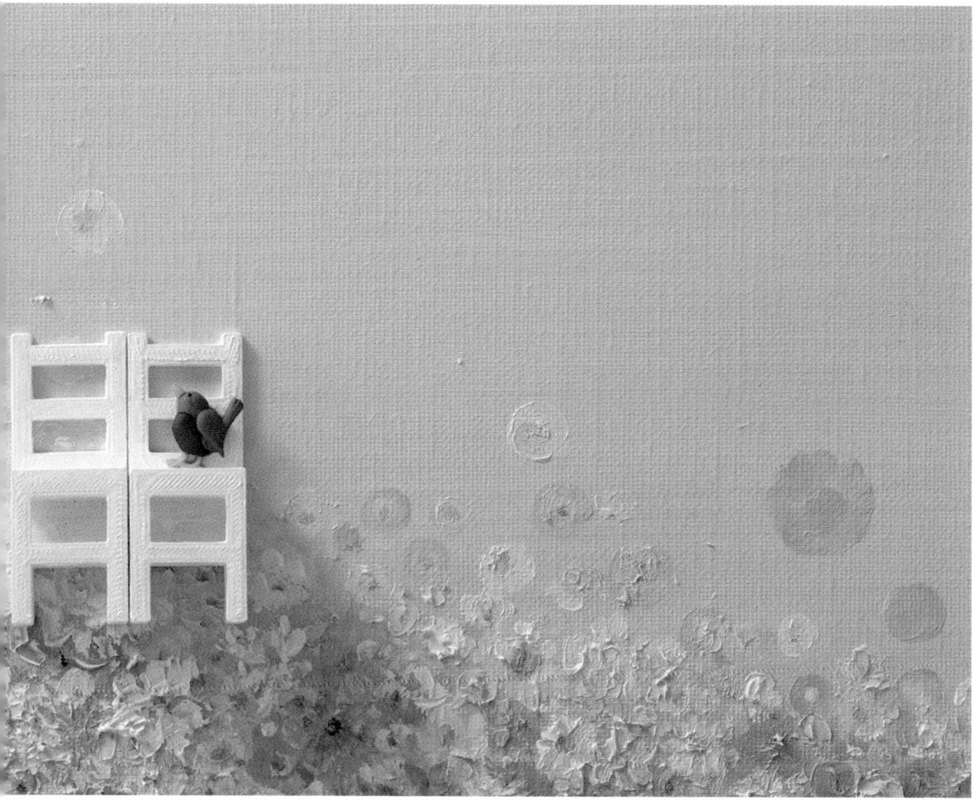

너에게 쓴다

꽃이 피었다고 너에게 쓰고
꽃이 졌다고 너에게 쓴다.
너에게 쓴 마음이
벌써 길이 되었다.
길 위에서 신발 하나 먼저 다 닳았다.

꽃 진 자리에 잎 피었다 너에게 쓰고
잎 진 자리에 새가 앉았다 너에게 쓴다.
너에게 쓴 마음이
벌써 내 일생이 되었다.
마침내 내 생生 풍화되었다.

—
천양희

Writing To You

Writing to you to say that the flower is blooming
And to say that the flower is withering.
My heart to you
Has become a path already.
A shoe wore out on this path.

Writing to you to say leaves are blooming where the flowers have withered
And where leaves have withered, a bird is resting.
My heart to you
Has become my life.
My life is weathered.

—
Chun Yang Hee

뒤편

성당의 종소리 끝없이 울려퍼진다
저 소리 뒤편에는
무수한 기도문이 박혀 있을 것이다

백화점 마네킹 앞모습이 화려하다
저 모습 뒤편에는
무수한 시침이 꽂혀 있을 것이다

뒤편이 없다면 생의 곡선도 없을 것이다

—
천양희

Rear Side

Cathedral's bell tolls
There are numerous prayers
Behind that sound

The department store mannequin is fancy
There are numerous stitches
At its rear

There would be no curves to life if there was no rear

—
Chun Yang Hee

어느 봄날

청소부 김씨
길을 쓸다가
간밤 떨어져내린 꽃잎 쓸다가
우두커니 서 있다
빗자루 세워두고, 빗자루처럼,
제 몸에 화르르 꽃물드는 줄도 모르고
불타는 영산홍에 취해서 취해서

그가 쓸어낼 수 있는 건
바람보다도 적다

—
나희덕

One Spring Day

A cleaner named Kim
Stands absentminded
After sweeping the street
Sweeping fallen petals from the night before
With the broomstick upright,
Unaware his body being soaked by petals much like that broomstick
Mesmerized by gleaming azaleas

What he can sweep
Is less than what the wind sweeps

—
HeeDuk Ra

꽃 앞에서

우주선을 만드는
첨단 과학도

생명의 향기
품고 있는

꽃 한 송이를
만들 수는 없으니.

세상의
어느 꽃 앞에서

발걸음 멈추고
생명의 신비를 느끼는

사람은
얼마나 행복한가

—
정연복

In Front Of A Flower

Even rocket science
That builds a spaceship

Cannot make
A single blossom of flower

That holds
The fragrance of life.

How happy
Is a person

Who pauses
In front of a flower

To marvel at the mystery of life

—
Jeong Yeon-bok

인생미로 人生美路

멈춰 설수록
더 멀리 갑니다

돌아볼수록
더 빨리 갑니다

함께 갈수록
더 쉽게 갑니다

빈손으로 갈수록
더 많이 얻습니다

길이 없을수록
더 많은 길이 열리는

인생은
미로[美路] 입니다

인생은
참 아름다운 길입니다

—
양광모

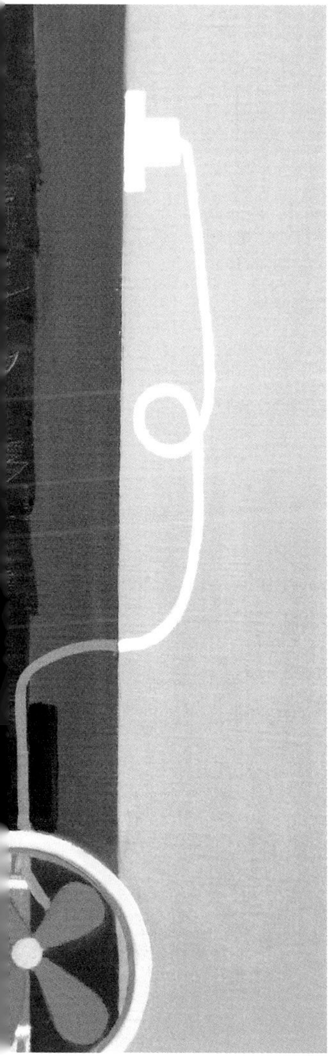

Beautiful Path Of Life

The more you stop
The further you go

The more you look back
The faster you go

The more you go together
The easier you go

The more empty-handed you go
The more you gain

The less paths there are
The more will open up

Life is such
A beautiful path

It is such
A lovely path

—
Yang Kwangmo

대추 한 알

저게 저절로 붉어질 리는 없다.
저 안에 태풍 몇 개
저 안에 천둥 몇 개
저 안에 벼락 몇 개

저게 저 혼자서 둥글어질 리는 없다.
저 안에 무서리 내리는 몇 밤
저 안에 땡볕 두어 달
저 안에 초승달 몇 날

—
장석주

One Date

That cannot mature on its own.
Within that, there are a few typhoons
A few thunders
A few thunderbolts

That cannot become formed on its own.
Within that, there are a few frosty nights
A month or two of sweltering heat
A few nights of crescents

—
Jang Seokju

내가 사랑하는 사람

나는 그늘이 없는 사람을 사랑하지 않는다
나는 그늘을 사랑하지 않는 사람을 사랑하지 않는다
나는 한 그루 나무의 그늘이 된 사람을 사랑한다
햇빛도 그늘이 있어야 맑고 눈이 부시다
나무 그늘에 앉아
나뭇잎 사이로 반짝이는 햇살을 바라보면
세상은 그 얼마나 아름다운가

나는 눈물이 없는 사람을 사랑하지 않는다
나는 눈물을 사랑하지 않는 사람을 사랑하지 않는다
나는 한 방울 눈물이 된 사람을 사랑한다
기쁨도 눈물이 없으면 기쁨이 아니다
사랑도 눈물 없는 사랑이 어디 있는가
나무 그늘에 앉아
다른 사람의 눈물을 닦아주는 사람의 모습은
그 얼마나 고요한 아름다움인가

—
정호승

Person That I Love

I do not love someone that does not have a shadow
I do not love someone that does not love a shadow
I love a person that became a shadow of a tree
Sunlight shines only if there is a shadow
How gorgeous is the world
When you see a gleaming sunlight between those leaves
Under the shadow

I do not love someone who has no tears
I do not love someone who does not love tears
I love a person that became a drop of tear
Joy is not a joy without sorrow
There is no love without sorrow
How beautiful is it
When one console another's sorrow
Under the shadow

—
Jeong Ho-seung

별똥별

별똥별이 떨어지는 순간에
내가 너를 생각하는 줄
넌 모르지

떨어지는 별똥별을 바라보는 순간에
내가 너의 눈물을 생각하는 줄
넌 모르지

내가 너의 눈물이 되어 떨어지는 줄
넌 모르지

—
정호승

Shooting Star

You won't know
That I think of you
The moment I see shooting stars

You won't know
That I think of your tears
The moment I see shooting stars

You won't know
That I become your tears and drop

—
Jeong Ho-seung

햇살에게

이른 아침에
먼지를 볼 수 있게 해주셔서 감사합니다
이제는 내가
먼지에 불과하다는 것을 알게 해주셔서 감사합니다
그래도 먼지가 된 나를
하루 종일
찬란하게 비춰주셔서 감사합니다

—
정호승

Dear Sunshine

Thank you for letting me
See dust in the early morning
Thank you for letting me
Realize that I am just a speck of dust
Despite so even if I am only dust,
Thank you for shining fulgently on me
All day long

—
Jeong Ho-seung

산유화

산에는 꽃 피네
꽃이 피네
갈 봄 여름없이
꽃이 피네.

산에
산에
피는 꽃은
저만치 혼자서 피어 있네.

산에서 우는 작은 새요
꽃이 좋아
산에서
사노라네.

산에는 꽃 지네
꽃이 지네
갈 봄 여름 없이
꽃이 지네.

—
김소월

Flowers In The Mountain

Flowers bloom in the mountain
Flowers bloom
Regardless of autumn, spring, and summer
Flowers bloom.

Flowers that bloom
In the mountain
In the mountain,
Bloomed alone, far out.

A bird
Crying in the mountain
Lives in the mountain
As it likes flowers.

Flowers wither in the mountain
Wither away
Regardless of autumn, spring, and summer
They wither away.

—
Kim Sowol

내 안에 머무는 그대

당신을 만나기 전에는
아침이 밝아왔는데
당신을 만난 후로는
사랑이 밝아옵니다

당신을 만나기 전에는
어둠이 밀려왔는데
당신을 만난 후로는
사랑이 밀려옵니다

아침부터 밤까지
내 안에 머무는 그대
당신을 만난 후로는
사랑 안에 내가 머뭅니다

—
양광모

You Dwell In Me

Before getting to know you
Morning had dawned
Since getting to know you
Love dawns

Before finding you
Darkness had surged
Since finding you
Love surges

All day and all night
You dwell in me
Since meeting you
I dwell in love

—
Yang Kwangmo

벗에게

너는
내 안에서
고운 잇속 드러내며
살짝 웃는다

이슬 달고 피어난
하얀 도라지 꽃

날마다
정성껏
너를 가꾼다

네가 꽃을 피워
나에겐
사랑이 되고

네가 살아와서
나의 눈물은
반짝이는 구슬이 된다

세월이 가도
젊음만 퍼 올리는
영혼의 샘가에서

순결한 눈짓 마주하여
피리 불다가
우리는 조용히
하나가 된다

—
이해인

Dear Friend

You
Smile slightly
Within me
Revealing your beautiful teeth

The white balloon flower
Bloomed with dew

Every day
I carefully
Adorn you

When you blossom flowers
They become love
To me

Because you came
My tears become
Sparkling beads

At the wellspring of the soul
That only brings youth
Even when time passes

We quietly
Become one
As we face each other with
innocent looks
While we play the flute

—
Claudia Lee Hae-in

2장

연연하다

To dwell on

6월

하루종일
당신 생각으로
6월의 나뭇잎에 바람이 불고
하루 해가 갑니다
불쑥불쑥 솟아나는
그대 보고 싶은 마음을
주저앉힐 수가 없습니다
창가에 턱을 괴고
오래오래 어딘가를 보고
있곤 합니다
느닷없이 그런 나를 발견하고는
그것이
당신 생각이었음을 압니다
하루종일
당신 생각으로
6월의 나뭇잎이
바람에 흔들리고
해가 갑니다.

—
김용택

June

All day goes by
Thinking of you
Wind caressing the leaves of June
I cannot subdue
The desire to long for you
Popping up abruptly
I tend to gaze somewhere
A long long time
With my chin on the windowsill
When I catch myself from doing so
I realize
It was all about you
All day goes by
Thinking of you
Leaves of June
Swaying in the wind.

—
Kim Yong Taek

Young Hee

다 당신입니다

개나리꽃이 피면 개나리 꽃 피는 대로
살구꽃이 피면은 살구꽃이 피는 대로
비 오면 비 오는 대로
그리워요
보고 싶어요
손잡고 싶어요
다

당신입니다

—
김용택

It's All You

When forsythia flower blooms, let it be
If apricot flower blooms, let it be
If it rains, let it be
I long for you
Miss you
Want to hold you

It's all you

—
Kim Yong Taek

사는 법

그리운 날은 그림을 그리고
쓸쓸한 날은 음악을 들었다

그리고도 남는 날은
너를 생각해야만 했다.

—
나태주

Way Of Living

The day I yearned, I drew pictures
The day I was lonely, I listened to music

The days that remained
I had to reminisce about you.

—
Tae-joo Na

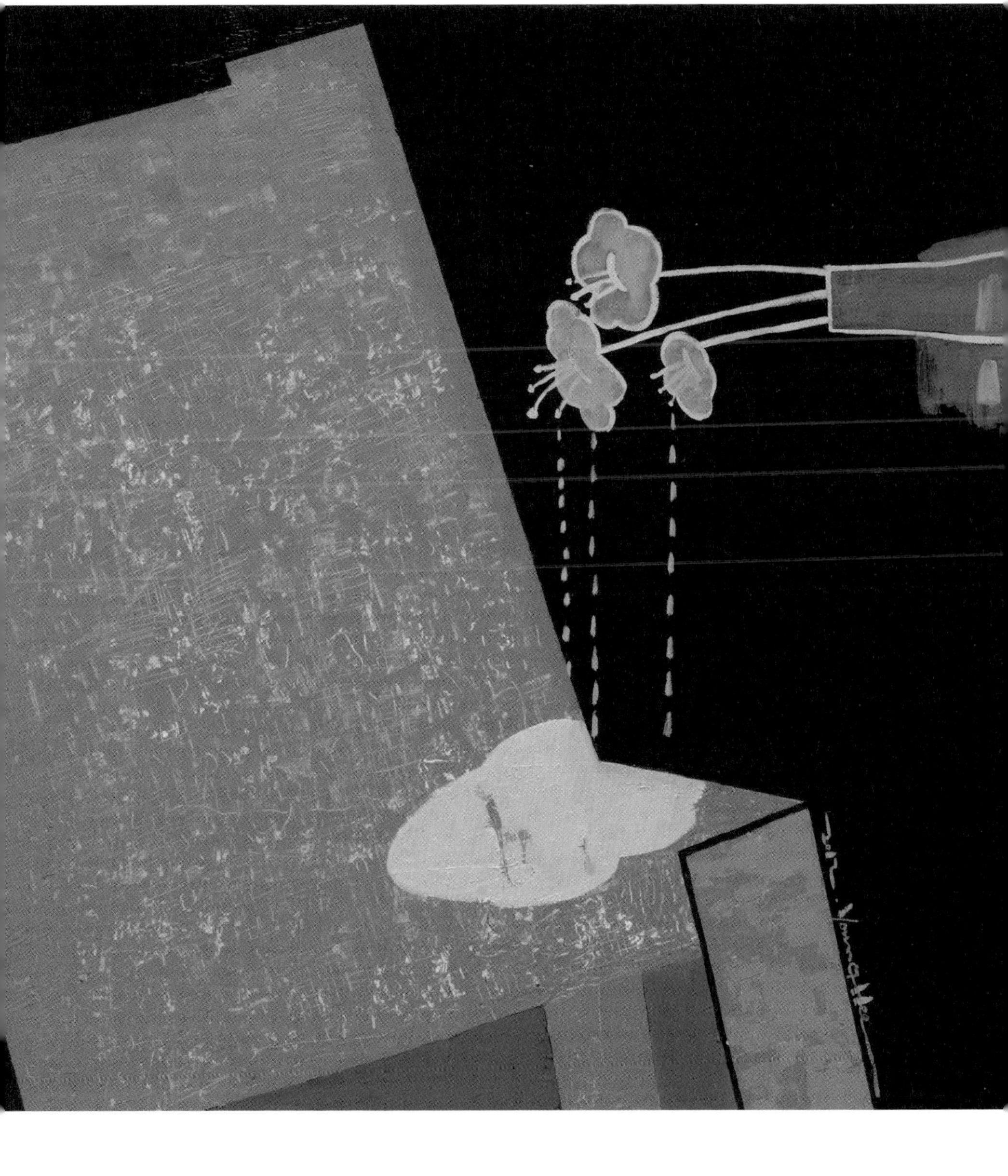

물안개

세월이 이따금 나에게 묻는다
사랑은 그 후 어떻게 되었느냐고
물안개처럼
몇 겁의 인연이란 것도
아주 쉽게 부서지더라

—
류시화

Wet Fog

Time is asking at times
What happened to the love thereafter
Aeons of ties
Also shatters very easily
Like a wet fog

—
Shiva Ryu

초겨울 편지

앞산에
고운 잎
다 졌답니다
빈 산을 그리며
저 강에
흰눈
내리겠지요

눈 내리기 전에
한번 보고 싶습니다

—
김용택

Early Winter Letter

Gorgeous leaves
On the mountain in front
Have all shed
It will probably snow
Over that river
Missing hollow mountain

I hope to see you
Before it snows

—
Kim Yong Taek

길 1

쓸쓸해져서야
보이는 풍경이 있다
버림받은 마음일 때에만
들리는 소리가 있다

새빨간 꽃 한 송이 피워
받들어 모시고
누구를 기다리는지
어여쁜 무덤이 하나

허리 아픈 사람처럼
꾸뭇거리다가
빗방울 두엇
새소리 몇 소절 함께
서둘러 마음속으로 숨어버리는
길이 있었다.

—
나태주

Path 1

There is a sight that you see
Only when you are forlorn
There is a sound that you hear
Only when you feel abandoned

A graceful grave
With a bright red flower
Carefully tending to it
Awaits someone

There is a path that
Wandered
Like a person with a sore back
Then hid away into the heart
With a few raindrops
And a few lines of birds singing.

—
Tae-joo Na

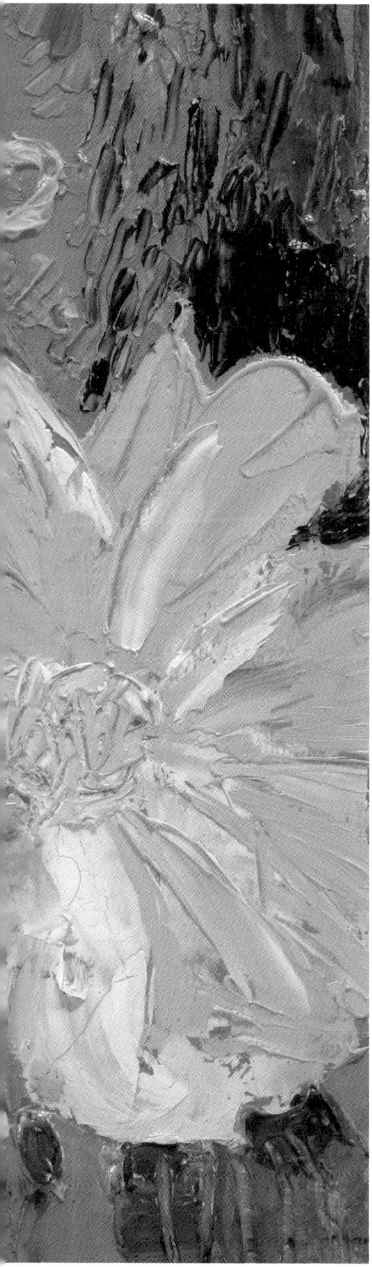

바람 부는 날

너는 내가 보고 싶지도 않니?
구름 위에 적는다

나는 너무 네가 보고 싶단다!
바람 위에 띄운다.

—
나태주

On A Windy Day

Do you not miss me?
I'm writing on a cloud

I miss you a lot!
I'm sending you my thoughts on that wind.

—
Tae-joo Na

시

그냥 줍는 것이다

길거리나 사람들 사이에
버려진 채 빛나는
마음의 보석들.

—
나태주

Poetry

It's just picking up

Jewels of heart
Shining while abandoned
Amongst people and streets.

—
Tae-joo Na

봄소식

봄이 온다기에
봄소식을 전하려 했더니
그대 마음은
아직도 겨울이었습니다

—
용혜원

Spring News

As spring is coming
I dared to deliver the spring news
However your heart was still
In the deep of winter

—
Yong Hye-Won

그 복숭아나무 곁으로

너무도 여러 겹의 마음을 가진
그 복숭아나무 곁으로
나는 왠지 가까이 가고 싶지 않았습니다
흰꽃과 분홍꽃을 나란히 피우고 서 있는 그 나무는 아마
사람이 앉지 못할 그늘을 가졌을 거라고
멀리로 멀리로만 지나쳤을 뿐입니다
흰꽃과 분홍꽃 사이에 수천의 빛깔이 있다는 것을
나는 그 나무를 보고 멀리서 알았습니다
눈부셔 눈부셔 알았습니다
피우고 싶은 꽃빛이 너무 많은 그 나무는
그래서 외로웠을 것이지만 외로운 줄도 몰랐을 것입니다
그 여러 겹의 마음을 읽는 데 참 오래 걸렸습니다

흩어진 꽃잎들 어디 먼 데 닿았을 무렵
조금은 심심한 얼굴을 하고 있는 그 복숭아나무 그늘에서
가만히 들었습니다 저녁이 오는 소리를

—
나희덕

Close To That Peach Tree

For some reason
I didn't want to get close to that peach tree
That has so many layers of emotions
I assumed that tree with white and pink blossoms
Has shade on which no one can sit
And only passed it from far far away
I realized by looking at that tree from a distance
That it has thousands of hues
Between layers of white and pink flowers
It was shining and gleaming so I knew
That tree with so many blossoms wanting to bloom
It would have been lonely because so
But it wouldn't have realized
It took forever to read those layers

By the time the scattered petals reached somewhere far
I peacefully listened under the shade of that resting peach tree
To the sound of dusk

—
HeeDuk Ra

수선화에게

울지 마라
외로우니까 사람이다
살아간다는 것은 외로움을 견디는 일이다
공연히 오지 않는 전화를 기다리지 마라
눈이 오면 눈길을 걸어가고
비가 오면 빗길을 걸어가라
갈대숲에서 가슴검은도요새도 너를 보고 있다
가끔은 하느님도 외로워서 눈물을 흘리신다
새들이 나뭇가지에 앉아 있는 것도 외로움 때문이고
네가 물가에 앉아 있는 것도 외로움 때문이다
산그림자도 외로워서 하루에 한 번씩 마을로 내려온다
종소리도 외로워서 울려퍼진다

—
정호승

Dear Daffodils

Do not weep
You are lonely as you are a human
Living through a life is about bearing loneliness
Do not vainly long for a phone call that will not ring
Walk through snowy path when it snows
Walk through rainy path when it rains
A snipe with a black chest is watching you in the reed forest
Even God also cries at times feeling lonely
Birds rest on branches because of loneliness
You also sit by the water because of loneliness
Mountain shadows come down over the village once a day
The sound of bell also resonates throughout because it's lonely

—
Jeong Ho-seung

술 한잔

인생은 나에게
술 한잔 사주지 않았다
겨울밤 막다른 골목 끝 포장마차에서
빈 호주머니를 털털 털어
나는 몇번이나 인생에게 술을 사주었으나
인생은 나를 위해 단 한번도
술 한잔 사주지 않았다
눈이 내리는 날에도
돌연꽃 소리없이 피었다 지는 날에도
인생은 나에게 술 한잔 사주지 않았다

—
정호승

A Drink

My life
Did not buy me a drink
I did several times
At the street vendor on winter nights
Emptying pocket
But my life not even once
Bought me a drink
Even on a snowy day
Or a day when flowers engraved on the stone silently bloom and wither
It never bought me a drink

—
Jeong Ho-seung

풀잎에도 상처가 있다

풀잎에도 상처가 있다
꽃잎에도 상처가 있다
너와 함께 걸었던 들길을 걸으면
들길에 앉아 저녁놀을 바라보면
상처 많은 풀잎들이 손을 흔든다
상처 많은 꽃잎들이
가장 향기롭다

—
정호승

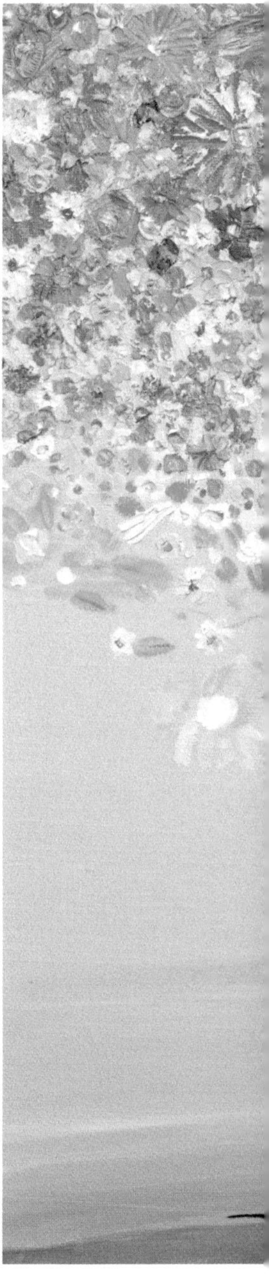

Blades Of Grass Also Have Scars

Blades of grass also have scars
Petals of flowers also have scars
As I walk along the trail that I walked with you
As I gaze at sunset sitting on the trail
The heavily scarred blades of grass wave at me
The heavily scarred petals of flowers
Are the most fragrant

—
Jeong Ho-seung

YoungHee

나 하나 꽃 피어

나 하나 꽃 피어
풀밭이 달라지겠느냐고
말하지 말아라
네가 꽃피고 나도 꽃피면
결국 풀밭이 온통
꽃밭이 되는 것 아니겠느냐

나 하나 물들어
산이 달라지겠느냐고도
말하지 말아라
내가 물들고 너도 물들면
결국 온 산이 활활
타오르는 것 아니겠느냐

—
조동화

By Me Blooming Alone

Do not ask
If a field would change
By me blooming alone
When you and I bloom
Isn't that
The whole field will eventually become a flower bed

Do not ask
If a mountain would change
By me tingeing alone
When you and I tinge
Isn't that
The entire mountain will eventually blaze

—
Jo Dong-hwa

저편 언덕

슬픔이 그대를 부를 때
고개를 돌리고
쳐다보라
세상의 어떤 것에도 의지 할 수 없을 때
그 슬픔에 기대라
저편 언덕처럼
슬픔이 그대를 손짓할 때
그곳으로 걸어가라
세상의 어떤 의미에도 기댈 수 없을 때
저편 언덕으로 가서
그대 자신에게 기대라
슬픔에 의지하되
다만 슬픔의 소유가 되지 말라

—
류시화

Over That Hill

When sorrow calls upon you
Turn around and
Face it
When there is nothing to rely on
Lean on that sorrow
When sorrow waves at you
Like that hill on the other side
Walk up to that place
When there is no purpose to lean on
Go over to the hill
Lean on yourself
Lean on sorrow
Though do not be possessed by it

—
Shiva Ryu

풀

풀이 눕는다
비를 몰아오는 동풍에 나부껴
풀은 눕고
드디어 울었다
날이 흐려서 더 울다가
다시 누웠다

풀이 눕는다
바람보다도 더 빨리 눕는다
바람보다도 더 빨리 울고
바람보다 먼저 일어난다

날이 흐리고 풀이 눕는다
발목까지
발밑까지 눕는다
바람보다 늦게 누워도
바람보다 먼저 일어나고
바람보다 늦게 울어도
바람보다 먼저 웃는다
날이 흐리고 풀뿌리가 눕는다

—
김수영

Grass

Grass lay down flat
Fluttered by the gush of east wind bringing rain
Grass lay flat
Then finally cried
Cried more because the weather was gloomy
Then laid flat again

Grass lay down flat
Lay faster than the wind
Cry faster than the wind
Get up faster than the wind

Grass lay flat in the gloomy weather
Down to an ankle
Down to the feet they lay
Even if they lay slower than the wind
They get up faster
Even if they cry slower than the wind
They smile faster than the wind
Weather is gloomy and grass roots lay down flat

—
Kim Su-Young

사랑한다는 것으로

사랑한다는 것으로
새의 날개를 꺾어
너의 곁에 두려 하지 말고
가슴에 작은 보금자리를 만들어
종일 지친 날개를
쉬고 다시 날아갈
힘을 줄 수 있어야 하리라

—
서정윤

Because You Love

Just because you love the bird
Do not clip its wing
To keep it by your side
Rather
Build a small nest in your heart
And help regain its strength
So that it can soar again

—
Seo Jeongyun

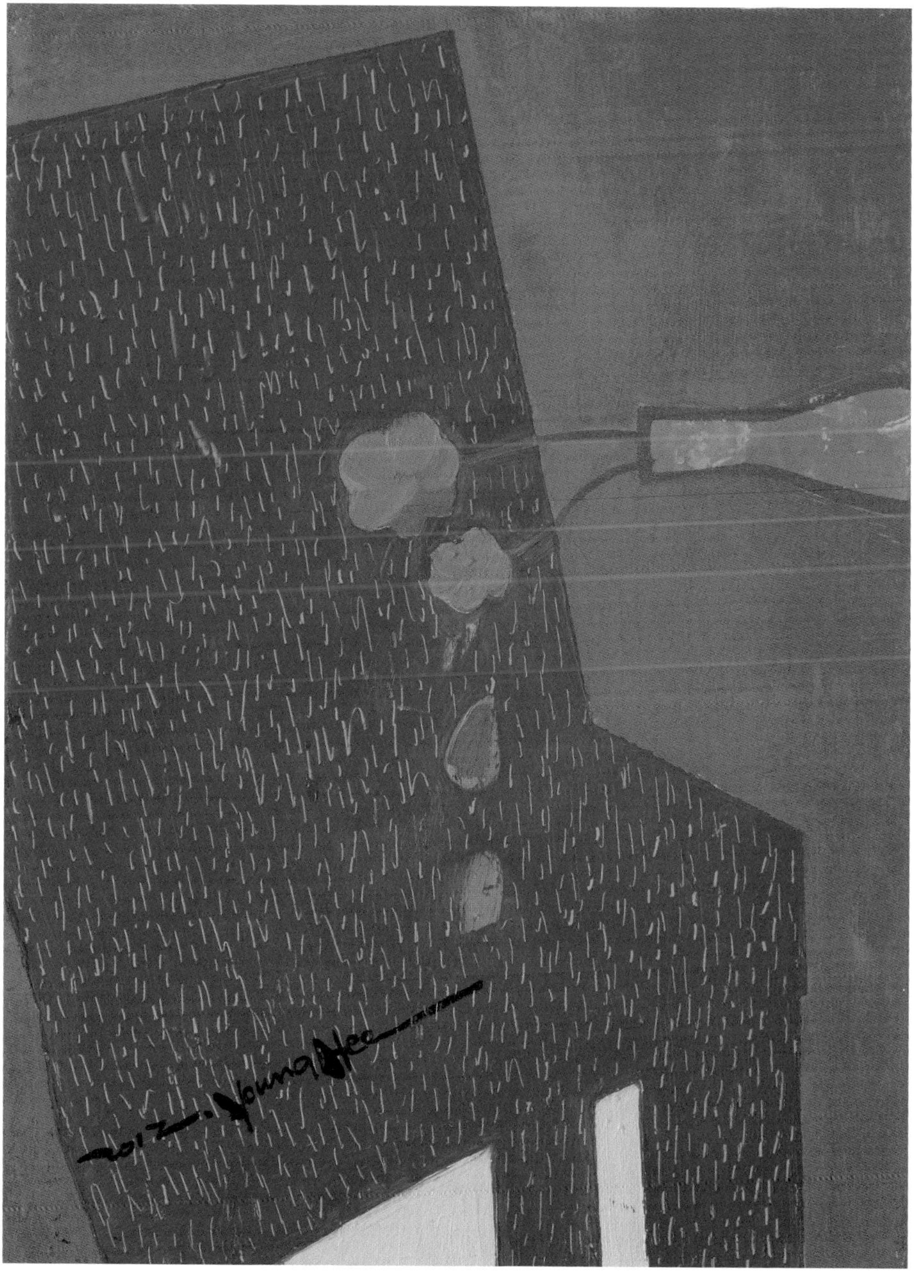

봄바람

봄철이 되어
봄바람이 쏴 분다.
세상이 온통 날라갈 것만 같다.

어쩌면
나는 당신을 사랑한다는 말이,
쉽게스리 풀려 나올 것 같다.

쉽게 말해서
오늘도 내일도 모레도,
봄바람이 한가하게 불었으면 한다.

—
천상병

Spring Wind

Spring is in the air
A spring breeze blows carelessly.
The whole world might blow away.

Perhaps
Saying I love you,
May be said more easily.

Simply said
I hope spring breeze continues leisurely
Today, tomorrow, and the day after.

—
Cheon Sang-byeong

괴산 가는 길

산 너머에 연기가
피어오르는 것을 보면

어머니,
하고 부른다

—
김초혜

On The Way To Town Guisan

When smoke puffs
Over the mountain

I call out
Mum

—
Kim Chohye

부모

낙엽이 우수수 떨어질 때,
겨울의 기나긴 밤,
어머님하고 둘이 앉아
옛이야기 들어라.

나는 어쩌면 생겨 나와
이 이야기 듣는가?
묻지도 말아라, 내일 날에
내가 부모 되어서 알아보랴?

—
김소월

Parents

When dried leaves flutter down,
Listen to old stories
Through the long, long winter night,
Sitting side by side with mum.

How was I born,
Now listening to these stories?
Don't even ask, in the near future
Do I know it when I myself become a parent?

—
Kim Sowol

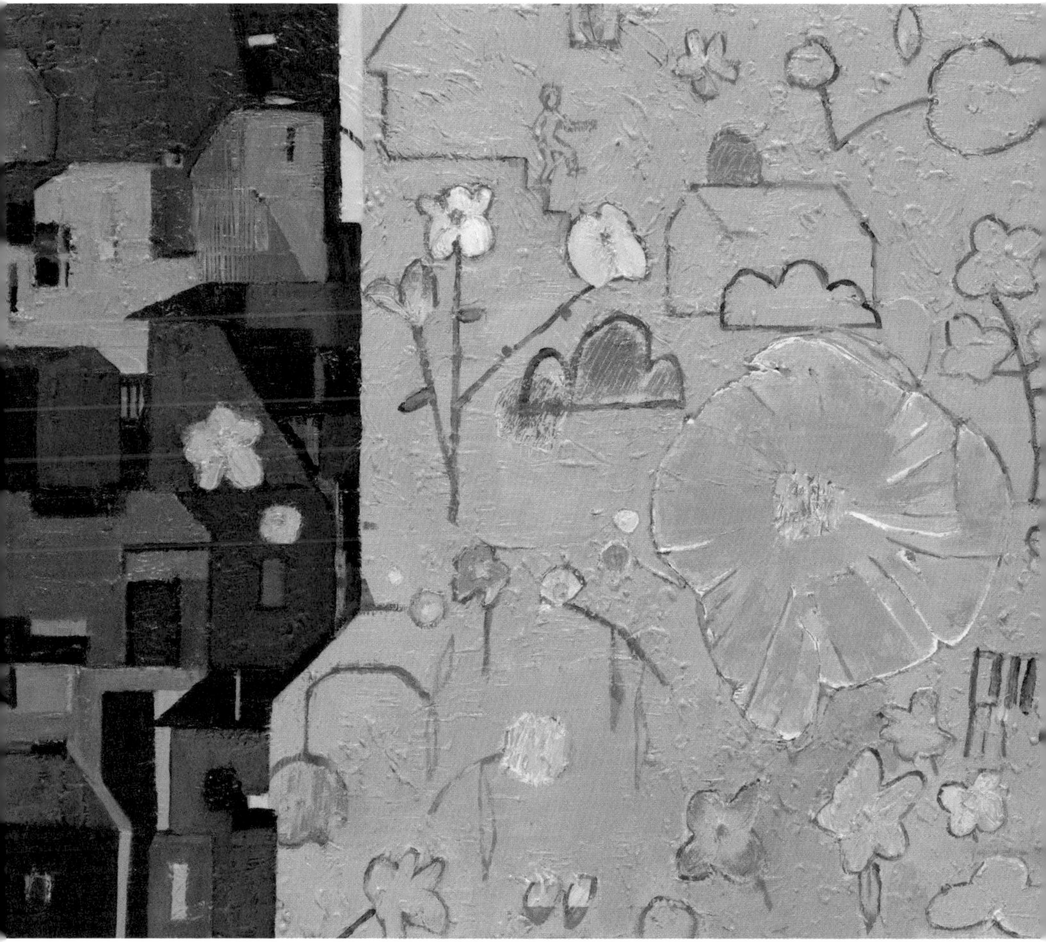

진달래꽃

나 보기가 역겨워
가실 때에는
말없이 고히 보내 드리우리다

영변에 약산
진달래꽃
아름따다 가실 길에 뿌리우리다

가시는 걸음걸음
놓인 그 꽃을
사뿐히 즈려밟고 가시옵소서

나 보기가 역겨워
가실 때에는
죽어도 아니 눈물 흘리우리다

—
김소월

Azalea Flower

When you can't stand the sight of me
And leave
I shall let you go without any objections

I shall pick myriad of azalea flowers
From Mt Yak in Youngbyun and
Sprinkle them on the path you take

Please leave
Trampling those flowers
On every step you take

When you can't stand the sight of me
And leave
I won't shed tears even beyond death

—
Kim Sowol

못잊어

못잊어 생각이 나겠지요,
그런대로 한세상 지내시구려,
사노라면 잊힐 날 있으리다.

못잊어 생각이 나겠지요,
그런대로 세월만 가라시구려,
못잊어도 더러는 잊히오리다.

그러나 또한긋 이렇지요,
'그리워 살뜰히 못 잊는데,
어쩌면 생각이 떠지나요?'

—
김소월

Can't Forget

I shall remember as I can't forget,
Just live the life as life shall flow,
If you live on, one day it shall be forgotten.

I shall remember as I can't forget,
Let the time pass,
Even if you can't forget all, some shall.

But having said this,
'How can I let go of the thought
When I can't sincerely forget because I miss so much?'

—
Kim Sowol

깊은 물

물이 깊어야 큰 배가 뜬다
얕은 물에는 술잔 하나 뜨지 못한다
이 저녁 그대 가슴엔 종이배 하나라도 뜨는가
돌아오는 길에도 시간의 물살에 쫓기는 그대는

얕은 물은 잔돌만 만나도 소란스러운데
큰 물은 깊어서 소리가 없다
그대 오늘은 또 얼마나 소리치며 흘러갔는가
굽이 많은 이 세상의 시냇가 여울을

—
도종환

Deep Water

Water must be deep for a big ship to float
Not even a shot glass can float in the shallow water
Can a paper boat be afloat in your heart
When you are being chased by time even at your return

In the shallow water it becomes noisy even with pebbles
But deep water is silent
How noisy were you today
Flowing through the curves of meandering stream

—
Do Jonghwan

다시 오는 봄

햇빛이 너무 맑아 눈물 납니다
살아 있구나 느끼니 눈물 납니다
기러기 떼 열 지어 북으로 가고
길섶에 풀들도 돌아오는데
당신은 가고 그리움만 남아서가 아닙니다
이렇게 살아 있구나 생각하니 눈물 납니다

—
도종환

Returning Spring

Dazzling sunlight brings tears to my eyes
Feeling alive brings tears to my eyes
A flock of wild geese line up to head north
Road verge greens up
Not because you are gone and only yearning is left behind
Realizing that I am alive brings tears to my eyes

—
Do Jonghwan

갈대

언제부턴가 갈대는 속으로
조용히 울고 있었다.
그런 어느 밤이었을 것이다. 갈대는
그의 온몸이 흔들리고 있는 것을 알았다.

바람도 달빛도 아닌 것.
갈대는 저를 흔드는 것이 제 조용한 울음인 것을
까맣게 몰랐다.
—산다는 것은 속으로 이렇게
조용히 울고 있는 것이란 것을
그는 몰랐다.

—
신경림

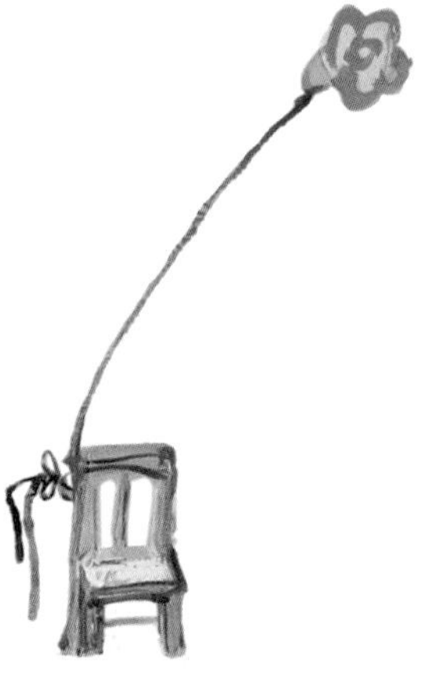

Reed

For sometime the reed has been crying
Quietly in its heart.
It would've been one night like that. The reed
Realized its whole body was swaying.

The reed did not realize
That what made them sway
Was not the wind nor moonlight but its quiet tears.
— It did not realize that
Being alive is
Crying silently like this.

—
Shin Kyeong-nim

2013. youngkoe

너에게 묻는다

연탄재 함부로 발로 차지 마라
너는
누구에게 한 번이라도 뜨거운 사람이었느냐

—
안도현

A Question For You

Do not kick at coal ashes
Have you
Ever been that warm to someone else

—
An Dohyeon

우리가 눈발이라면

우리가 눈발이라면
허공에서 쭈빗쭈빗 흩날리는
진눈깨비는 되지 말자
세상이 바람 불고 춥고 어둡다 해도
사람이 사는 마을
가장 낮은 곳으로
따뜻한 함박눈이 되어 내리자
우리가 눈발이라면
잠 못 든 이의 창문가에서는
편지가 되고
그이의 깊고 붉은 상처 위에 돋는
새 살이 되자

—
안도현

If We Were Snow

If we were snow
Let's not be sleet
That coyly dissipate and scatter
Though the world may be windy, cold and dark
Let's be snowflakes
That land at the lowest part of the village where people are
If we were snow
Let's become a letter
At windowsills of those that are sleepless
Let's be a newly formed flesh
That heals over his deep red wounds

—
An Dohyeon

바람이 불어

바람이 어디로부터 불어와
어디로 불려 가는 것일까,

바람이 부는데
내 괴로움에는 이유가 없다.

내 괴로움에는 이유가 없을까,

단 한 여자를 사랑한 일도 없다.
시대를 슬퍼한 일도 없다.

바람이 자꾸 부는데
내 발이 반석 위에 섰다.

강물이 자꾸 흐르는데
내 발이 언덕 위에 섰다.

—
윤동주

Wind Blows

Where does the wind come from
And where does it go,

Wind blows
There is no reason for my distress.

Is there no reason for my distress,

Never loved a woman.
Nor mourned over an era.

Wind is blowing continuously
My feet are on the solid rock.

River is flowing continuously
My feet are on the hill.

—
Yun Dong-Ju

소낙비

번개, 뇌성, 왁자지근 뚜드려
머언 도회지에 낙뢰가 있어만 싶다.

벼룻장 엎어논 하늘로
살 같은 비가 살처럼 쏟아진다.

손바닥만 한 나의 정원이
마음같이 흐린 호수되기 일쑤다.

바람이 팽이처럼 돈다.
나무가 머리를 이루 잡지 못한다.

내 경건한 마음을 모셔 들여
노아 때 하늘을 한 모금 마시다.

—
윤동주

Shower

Thunder, lightning thud chaotically
It feels like there needs to be a thunderbolt in the city afar.

The sky as dark as spilt black ink
Raindrops like arrows, pours down like arrows.

My palm-sized garden
Becomes a murky lake like my heart.

The tornado spins like a top.
The trees cannot grasp their heads.

Take in my devout heart
And like Noah, drink a sip of the sky.

—
Yun Dong-Ju

청포도

내 고장 칠월은
청포도가 익어가는 시절

이 마을 전설이 주절이주절이 열리고
먼데 하늘이 꿈꾸며 알알이 들어와 박혀

하늘 밑 푸른 바다가 가슴을 열고
흰 돛단배가 곱게 밀려서 오면

내가 바라는 손님은 고달픈 몸으로
청포를 입고 찾아온다고 했으니

내 그를 맞아 이 포도를 따먹으면
두 손은 함뿍 적셔도 좋으련

아이야 우리 식탁엔 은쟁반에
하이얀 모시 수건을 마련해 두렴

—
이육사

Green Grapes

July in my hometown
Is the season for maturing green grapes

When the village's legends open one by one
Sky plunging into beads dreaming afar

Blue ocean under the sky opens up the heart
A white sailing boat gets pushed in swiftly

My companion I have been longing for
Should arrive in a bluish hemp robe

When I pick these grapes as I greet him(her)
I'd be glad to have my hands wet

Child, make ready a white linen towel
On the silver tray on the table

—
Lee Yuksa

첫 사랑

그대가 꺾어준 꽃,
시들 때까지 들여다보았네

그대가 남기고 간 시든 꽃
다시 필 때까지

—
이윤학

First Love

I've gazed at the flower you gave me
Until it withered

Until the withered flower you've left behind
Blooms again

—
Lee Yoonhak

의자

병원에 갈 채비를 하며
어머니께서
한 소식 던지신다

허리가 아프니까
세상이 다 의자로 보여야
꽃도 열매도, 그게 다
의자에 앉아 있는 것이여

주말엔
아버지 산소 좀 다녀와라
그래도 큰애 네가
아버지한테는 좋은 의자 아녔냐

이따가 침 맞고 와서는
참외밭에 지푸라기도 깔고
호박에 똬리도 받쳐야겠다
그것들도 식군데 의자를 내줘야지

싸우지 말고 살아라
결혼하고 애 낳고 사는 게 별거냐
그늘 좋고 풍경 좋은 데다가
의자 몇 개 내놓는 거여

—
이정록

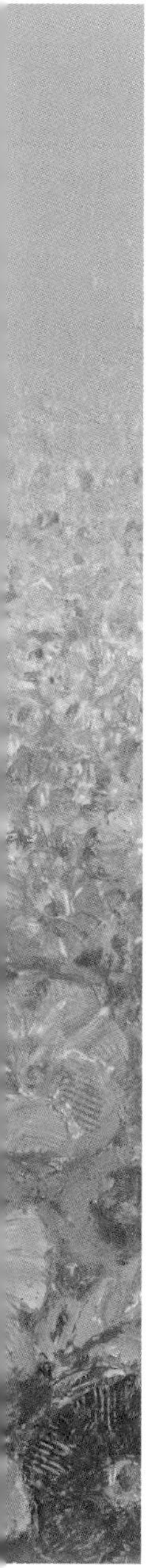

Chair

As mum gets ready to leave for hospital
She tells me something

All I see in this world are chairs
Due to my back pain
From flowers to fruits, everything
Rests on a chair

Go and visit your father's grave this weekend
Nonetheless
You were a strong support for you father like a chair

I should cover the melon field with straws
And place cushion on pumpkins after getting my acupuncture
They are also our family
And should be provided with seats to rest

Don't fight
Getting married and having kids are just a way of life
Just pull out some seats
Under the shade and enjoy the view

—
Lee Jungrok

여백이 있는 날

휴식과 사색이 마련될 수 있는 날
평소에 무심이 지나쳤던
자연과 사물과 사람을
제대로 유심히 바라보며
마음의 문을 열 수 있는
여백이 있는 날

—
이해인

Unmapped Day

A day for rest and brown study
To muse over nature, objects and people
Overlooked
Ordinary
An unmapped day
When a soul can open his mind

—
Claudia Lee Hae-in

향수

넓은 벌 동쪽 끝으로
옛이야기 지줄대는 실개천이 휘돌아나가고,
얼룩백이 황소가
해설피[해질 무렵] 금빛 게으른 울음을 우는 곳,

— 그곳이 차마 꿈엔들 잊힐 리야.

질화로에 재가 식어지면
비인 밭에 밤바람 소리 말을 달리고,
엷은 졸음에 겨운 늙으신 아버지가
짚베개를 돋아 고이시는 곳,

— 그곳이 차마 꿈엔들 잊힐 리야.

흙에서 자란 내 마음
파아란 하늘빛이 그리워
함부로 쏜 화살을 찾으러
풀섶 이슬에 함추름 휘적시던 곳,

— 그곳이 차마 꿈엔들 잊힐 리야.

Nostalgia

Home where
A rill full of folktales whirls around
At the east end of prairie,
Brindle cows moo in vain at golden sunset,

- Cannot be forgotten even in my dreams.

Home where
Night wind blows in a vast field with the sound of galloping horses
When ashes in mud furnace cool down,
Old father leans on straw stack as a pillow as he dozes off lightly,

- Cannot be forgotten even in my dreams.

Home where
I get soaked in wet grass
While looking for the arrow that I drew carelessly as
My heart born on earth longs for the heaven,

- Cannot be forgotten even in my dreams.

전설바다에 춤추는 밤물결 같은
검은 귀밑머리 날리는 어린 누이와
아무렇지도 않고 예쁠 것도 없는
사철 발 벗은 아내가
따가운 햇살을 등에 지고 이삭 줍던 곳,

— 그곳이 차마 꿈엔들 잊힐 리야.

하늘에는 성근* 별
알 수도 없는 모래성으로 발을 옮기고,
서리 까마귀 우지짖고 지나가는 초라한 지붕,
흐릿한 불빛에 돌아앉아 도란도란거리는 곳,

— 그곳이 차마 꿈엔들 잊힐 리야.

—
정지용

* 성근: 여러 모양의 별들이 섞여 빛나는 모습

Home where
Young sister with dark short hair dancing like ocean waves
And wife who is indifferent and is not anything pretty
Were busy gleaning under the glaring sun,

- Cannot be forgotten even in my dreams.

Home where
Galaxies in the sky travel into unknown milk way,
Crying crow flies over the shabby roof,
People under the dim light and tell stories,

- Cannot be forgotten even in my dreams.

—
Chong Chi-Yong

비

돌에
그늘이 차고,

따로 몰리는
소소리 바람.

앞서거니 하여
꼬리 치날리어 세우고,

종종 다리 까칠한
산새 걸음걸이.

여울 지어
수척한 흰 물살,

갈갈이
손가락 펴고.

멎은 듯
새삼 도는 빗낱

붉은 잎 잎
소란히 밟고 간다.

—
정지용

Rain

Shadow
Darkens over the stone,

Sharp wind
Blows from the opposite side.

Rushing before the wind
With its tail tall and high,

Light legged
With bristly long thin legs.

Converged fords
Emaciated white current,

Hands wide open
With fingers apart,

Raindrops falling
As if stopped drop by drop

Tapping on
Every red leaves boisterously.

—
Chong Chi-Yong

풍경 달다

운주사 와불님을 뵙고
돌아오는 길에
그대 가슴의 처마 끝에
풍경을 달고 돌아왔다
먼데서 바람 불어와
풍경 소리 들리면
보고 싶은 내 마음이
찾아간 줄 알아라

—
정호승

Wind Bell

On my way back
After seeing Buddha at Unju temple
I hung a wind bell
On your heart
If the wind blows from afar
And you hear the sound of the wind bell
That will be my longing heart
Searching for you

—
Jeong Ho-seung

귀천

나 하늘로 돌아가리라
새벽빛 와 닿으면 스러지는
이슬 더불어 손에 손을 잡고,

나 하늘로 돌아가리라.
노을빛 함께 단둘이서
기슭에서 놀다가 구름 손짓하며는,

나 하늘로 돌아가리라.
아름다운 이 세상 소풍 끝내는 날,
가서, 아름다웠더라고 말하리라……

—
천상병

Return To Heaven

I will return to heaven
Along with the morning dew
That scatters as dawn arises,

I will return to heaven.
When the clouds call upon
After playing around with the twilight at the banks,

I will return to heaven.
On the day when a picnic to this beautiful world is over,
I will return, and tell them that it was beautiful……

—
Cheon Sang-byeong

강물이 흐르며

먼저 가려고 다투지도 않고
뒤에 쳐져 온다고 꾸짖지도 않는다.
앞서 간다고 뽐낼 줄도 모르고
뒤에 간다고 애탈 것도 없다.

먼 길을 가자면
서둘러도 안 되고
조바심해도 안 된다는 걸 안다.
제 차례를 지키며 쉬지 않고 간다.

가는 길에 낯선 물이 끼어들면
싫다 않고 받아 준다.
금방 만나도 한마음이 된다.
마음이 넓어서 자리다툼도 없다.

지구가 태양 둘레를 쉬지 않고 돌듯
세월 따라 쉬지 않고 흐른다.
잠이 오면 자면서 흐른다.

패랭이꽃도 만나고
아름다운 새들의 노래가 꾀어도
한눈팔지 않고 갈 길을 간다.
큰일을 위해 참고 견딜 줄 안다.

—
최춘해

As River Flows

It does not argue to be the first
Nor rage even as it lags.
It does not boast for being forward
Nor agonize for being behind.

It knows it shouldn't rush
To reach afar
Safe and sound.
It keeps flowing without stopping, keeping its order.

When unfamiliar water intervenes
It lets in without hate.
It quickly becomes in accord when they meet.
There is no disagreement about a seat.

Just like the Earth that orbits around the Sun endlessly
It flows continuously with time.
When exhausted, it flows asleep.

Even it swings by rainbow pink flowers
And is tempted by the lovely songs of birds
It flows without being distracted.
It knows to endure for a great cause.

—
Choi Chunhae

사랑

봄물보다 깊으니라
갈산보다 높으니라
달보다 빛나리라
돌보다 굳으리라
사랑을 묻는 이 있거든
이대로만 말하리

—
한용운

Love

It's deeper than the spring water
Higher than the fall mountain
Brighter than the moon
Firmer than the rock
If anyone asks what love is
Say this is so

—
Han Yong-un

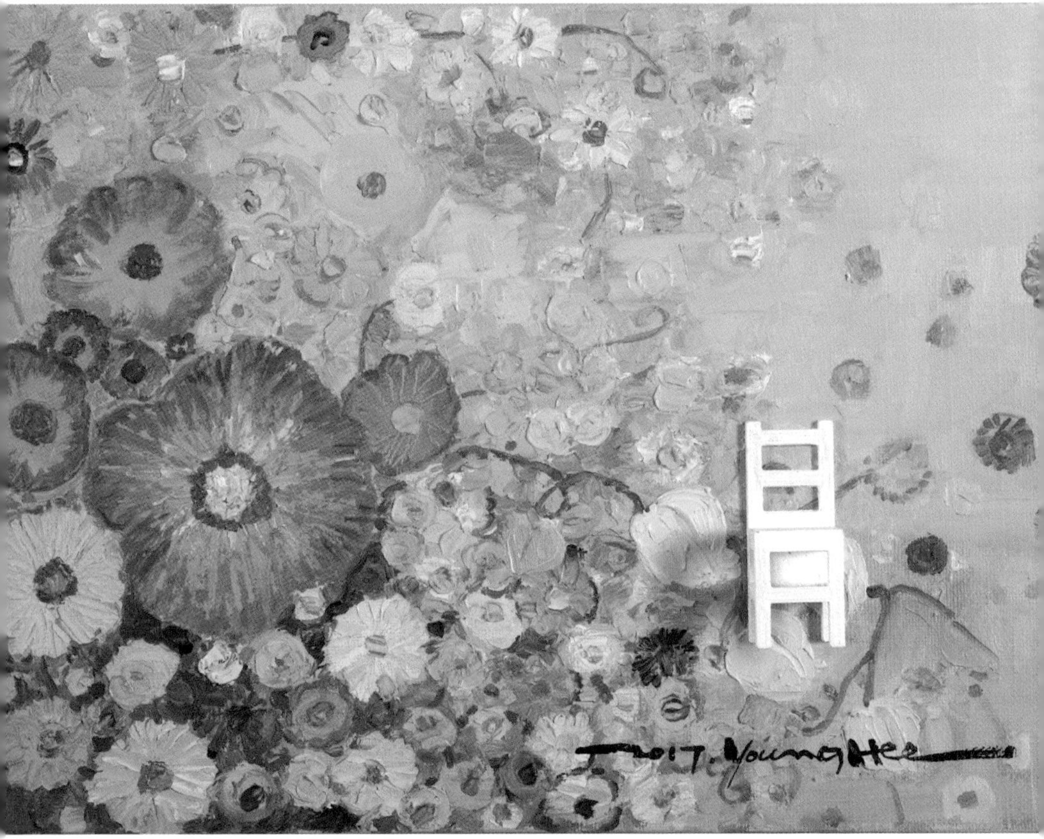
2017. YoungHee

가을

당신 생각을 켜놓은 채 잠이 들었습니다

—
함민복

Autumn

I fell asleep with the thought of you turned on

—
Ham Min Bok

깨끗한 빗자루

세상의 묵은 때들 적시며 씻겨주려고
초롱초롱 환하다 봄비
너 지상의 맑고 깨끗한 빗자루 하나

—
박남준

A Clean Broomstick

To wet and sweep old stubborn stains of the world
Twinkling spring rain shimmers
A pristine and clean broom stick of the earth

—
Park Namjoon

3장

성찰하다

To reflect on

눈
Snow

사과
Apple

서시
Prelude

선운사에서
At Sunwoon Temple

조용한 일
A Silent Thing

어부
Fisherman

한줄로 살아보라
Live On One Sentence

그 말
That Saying

꽃그늘
Flower Shade

멀리서 빈다
Wishing From Afar

안부
Call

풀 꽃 2
A Wild Flower 2

서시
Prelude

6월에 꿈꾸는 사랑
Love In June

이 순간
This Moment

새와 나무
A Bird And A Tree

느림의 열정
Passion

땅
Land

시멘트
Cement

겨울사랑
Winter Love

그대에게 가는 길
The Way To You

벚꽃 잎
Cherry Blossom

산속에서
In The Mountain

서시
Prelude

실수한 후
After Stumbling

술에 취한 바다
Boozed Ocean

내 마음은
My Heart Is

가는 길
On The Way

엄마야 누나야
Mum and Sis

예전엔 미처 몰랐어요
I Didn't Quite Know Before

돌담에 속삭이는 햇발
Sunshine Whispering Into
The Stonewall

모란이 피기까지는
Until The Peonies Bloom

나그네
Wayfarer

기도 1
Prayer 1

나의 어머니
My Mother

지란지교 를 꿈꾸며
Wishing A Noble and
Eternal Friendship

불행
Unhappiness

산
Mountain

호수
Lake

희망
Hope

신년 시
New Year's Greetings

하늘
The Sky

님의 침묵
Silence Of My Beloved

사랑하는 까닭
Reason For Love

나의 소망
My Wish

눈

지난밤에
눈이 소오복이 왔네

지붕이랑
길이랑 밭이랑
추워한다고
덮어 주는 이불인가봐

그러기에
추운 겨울에만 나리지

—
윤동주

Snow

It snowed beautifully
Last night

It must be a cozy blanket
For the roof, the road and the field
Left out
In the cold

That's why
It only snows in cold winter

—
Yun Dong-Ju

사과

붉은 사과 한 개를
아버지, 어머니,
누나, 나, 넷이서
껍질째로 송치까지
다- 노나 먹었소.

1936년 12월추정

—
윤동주

Apple

We shared
A red apple
Its skin and core
Four of us
Dad, mum, sister and me.

December 1936est

—
Yun Dong-Ju

서시

죽는 날까지 하늘을 우르러
한점 부끄럼이 없기를,
잎새에 이는 바람에도
나는 괴로워했다.
별을 노래하는 마음으로
모든 죽어가는것을 사랑해야지
그리고 나한테 주어진 길을
거러가야겠다.

오늘밤에도 별이 바람에 스치운다.

—
윤동주

Prelude

I hope to have no shame
When I look up to heaven until my death,
I was distressed
By the wind blowing on a leaf.
I will love all the mortals
With the heart full of starry songs
And I shall follow
My given path.

Tonight, wind blows again gently against the stars.

—
Yun Dong-Ju

선운사에서

꽃이
피는 건 힘들어도
지는 건 잠깐이더군
골고루 쳐다볼 틈 없이
님 한번 생각할 틈 없이
아주 잠깐이더군

그대가 처음
내 속에 피어날 때처럼
잊는 것 또한 그렇게
순간이면 좋겠네

멀리서 웃는 그대여
산 넘어 가는 그대여

꽃이
지는 건 쉬워도
잊는 건 한참이더군
영영 한참이더군

—
최영미

At Sunwoon Temple

It's difficult for a flower
To bloom
But was brief to wither
No moment to spare to look thoroughly
No time to spare to think of you
It was very brief

Wish forgetting is also
As brief
Like the time
When you start to bloom in me

Thee smiling from afar
Beyond mountain valleys

It's easy for a flower
To wither
But takes a long time to forget
Takes forever and ever

—
Choi Youngmi

조용한 일

이도 저도 마땅치 않은 저녁
철이른 낙엽 하나 슬며시 곁에 내린다

그냥 있어볼 길밖에 없는 내 곁에
저도 말없이 그냥 있는다

고맙다
실은 이런 것이 고마운 일이다

—
김사인

A Silent Thing

One awkward evening
An early autumn leaf falls down quietly by me

It has no option but to stay by me
It stays silently without a word

Thank you
Frankly, things like this are something to be grateful for

—
Kim Sa-in

'18. Young Hee

어부

바닷가에 매어둔
작은 고깃배
날마다 출렁거린다
풍랑에 뒤집힐 때도 있다
화사한 날을 기다리고 있다
머얼리 노를 저어 나가서
헤밍웨이의 바다와 노인이 되어서
중얼거리려고

살아온 기적이 살아갈 기적이 된다고
사노라면
많은 기쁨이 있다고

—
김종삼

Fisherman

A fishing boat
Tied by the shore
Rocks everyday
Flips over at times by storm
Awaits for a sunny day
To row afar
Like that Hemingway's Sea and The Old Man
And mumble

That miracle of having been alive will be the miracle to live on
If you live on
There shall be abundance of joy

—
Kim Chongsam

한줄로 살아보라

한줄의 글을 쓰고 나면
나는 다른 땅을 밟고 있었다.
내가 낯설었다.
낯선 내 얼굴이
나는 좋았다.
그가 나를 보며
나직이 말했다.
살아보라.

—
김용택

Live On One Sentence

I stood on a different land
When I wrote a sentence.
I felt strange.
I liked
My unfamiliar face.
He gazed at me
And spoke softly.
Live on.

—
Kim Yong Taek

그 말

보고 싶었다
많이 생각이 났다

그러면서도 끝까지
남겨두는 말은
사랑한다
너를 사랑한다

입속에 남아서 그 말
꽃이 되고
향기가 되고
노래가 되기를 바란다.

—
나태주

That Saying

Missed you
Couldn't stop thinking about you

But even still, until the end
The words left behind are
Love you
I love you

That saying, left inside the mouth
Hope it becomes a flower
A scent
And a song.

—
Tae-joo Na

꽃그늘

아이한테 물었다

이담에 나 죽으면
찾아와 울어줄 거지?

대답 대신 아이는
눈물 고인 두 눈을 보여주었다.

—
나태주

Flower Shade

Asked a child

Will you come and cry for me
When I die?

Instead of a response
The child showed me eyes filled with tears.

—
Tae-joo Na

멀리서 빈다

어딘가 내가 모르는 곳에
보이지 않는 꽃처럼 웃고 있는
너 한 사람으로 하여 세상은
다시 한 번 눈부신 아침이 되고

어딘가 네가 모르는 곳에
보이지 않는 풀잎처럼 숨 쉬고 있는
나 한 사람으로 하여 세상은
다시 한 번 고요한 저녁이 온다

가을이다, 부디 아프지 마라.

—
나태주

Wishing From Afar

Somewhere I don't know
Smiling like an invisible flower
Because of you, the world
Becomes a bright morning once again

Somewhere you don't know
Breathing like an invisible grass leaf
Because of me, the world
Becomes a silent dusk once again

It's autumn, don't be sick.

—
Tae-joo Na

안부

오래
보고 싶었다

오래
만나지 못했다

잘 있노라니
그것만 고마웠다.

—
나태주

Call

Have been longing
For a long time

Haven't been able to meet up
For a long time

It was grateful to hear
That you are well.

—
Tae-joo Na

풀 꽃 2

이름을 알고 나면 이웃이 되고
색깔을 알고 나면 친구가 되고
모양까지 알고 나면 연인이 된다
아, 이것은 비밀.

—
나태주

A Wild Flower 2

Once you know its name, it becomes a neighbour
Once you know its color, it becomes a friend
Once you know even its shape, it becomes a lover
Oh, This is a secret.

—
Tae-joo Na

서시

마을이 가까울수록
나무는 흠집이 많다.

내 몸이 너무 성하다.

—
이정록

Prelude

The closer the trees are to the villages
The more divots they have.

My body is too clean.

—
Lee Jungrok

6월에 꿈꾸는 사랑

사는 일이 너무 바빠
봄이 간 후에야 봄이 온 줄 알았네
청춘도 이와 같아
꽃만 꽃이 아니고
나 또한 꽃이었음을
젊음이 지난 후에야 젊음인 줄 알았네

인생이 길다 한들
천년만년 살 것이며
인생이 짧다 한들
가는 세월 어찌 막으리

봄은 늦고 여름은 이른
6월 같은 사람들아
피고 지는 이치가
어디 꽃뿐이라 할까

—
이채

Love In June

Living a busy life
I realized spring only after it passed by
Youthful days were the same
Not only the flowers were flowers
But I too were a flowers
I realized my youthful days only after it passed by

Even if life is long
How would you live thousands of years
Even if life is short
How could you resist time that flies

Dear those who are like the month of June
Who are too late to be spring, too early to be summer
This cycle of blooming and withering
Sits beyond flowers

—
Lee Chae

이 순간

이 순간 내가
별들을 쳐다본다는 것은
그 얼마나 화려한 사실인가

오래지 않아
내 귀가 흙이 된다 하더라도
이 순간 내가
제 9 교향곡을 듣는다는 것은
그 얼마나 찬란한 사실인가

그들이 나를 잊고
내 기억 속에서 그들이 없어진다 하더라도
이 순간 내가
친구들과 웃고 이야기한다는 것은
그 얼마나 즐거운 사실인가

두뇌가 기능을 멈추고
내 손이 썩어가는 때가 오더라도
이 순간 내가
마음 내키는 대로 글을 쓰고 있다는 것은
허무도 어찌하지 못할 사실이다

—
피천득

This Moment

How gorgeous is it
Looking at stars
At this moment

How splendid is it
Listening to Symphony No. 9
At this moment
Even though my ears
Will eventually become earth

How exciting is it
Being able to talk and laugh
With friends
At this moment
Even if they forget me and I forget them

Futility can't interrupt the fact
That I am writing the way I want to
At this moment
Even if the day eventually comes
Where my brain will stop working and hands die away

—
Pi Chundeuk

새와 나무

여기 바람 한 점 없는 산속에 서면
나무들은 움직임 없이 고요한데
어떤 나뭇가지 하나만 흔들린다
그것은 새가
그 위에 날아와 앉았기 때문이다
별일 없이 살아가는 뭇사람들 속에서
오직 나만 홀로 흔들리는 것은
당신이
내 안에 날아와 앉았기 때문이다
새는 그 나뭇가지에 집을 짓고
나무는 더 이상 흔들리지 않지만
나만 홀로 끝없이 흔들리는 것은
당신이 내 안에 집을 짓지 않은 까닭이다

—
류시화

A Bird And A Tree

In this mountain where there is no breeze
Trees are still and silent
Yet a branch sways
It's because a bird
Alighted on it
The reason I sway
In the midst of people living through everyday norms
Is because
You alighted in me
The tree no longer sways
As the bird builds its nest on that branch
But I still sway alone endlessly
Because you have not built a home within me

—
Shiva Ryu

느림의 열정

이 바쁜 세상에
누가 꽃이 더디 핀다 하는가
이 빠른 세상에
누가 나무가 느리다 하는가

꽃은 서두르지 않는다
나무는 게으르지 않는다
삶은 결코 비교되지 않는다

하루하루 최선을 다해
자기만의 리듬으로 피어나는
치열한 느림의 열정일 뿐

—
박노해

Passion

Who said that the flower blossoms
Drag in this busy world
Who said that the trees
Are slow in this speedy world

No flowers hurry
No trees dawdle
No lives can be compared

It's simply a fierce passion in a gradual pace
Blooming at its own rate
By giving its best day by day

—
Park Nohae

땅

모든것을 품고도
모든것 아래에 있는
가장 겸손한 그대

—
서윤덕

Land

Bears all
Below all
Most humble of all

—
Seo Yoon Duk

시멘트

부드러운 것이 강하다
자신이 가루가 될 때까지 철저하게
부서져본 사람만이 그것을 안다

—
유용주

Cement

What is soft is strong
Only those who have been ground down
Into the finest powder know that

—
Yu Yongjoo

겨울사랑

눈송이처럼 너에게 가고 싶다
머뭇거리지 말고
서성대지 말고
숨기지 말고
그냥 네 하얀 생애속에 뛰어들어
따스한 겨울이 되고 싶다
천년 백설이 되고 싶다

—
문정희

Winter Love

I would like to come to you like a snowflake
Without hesitation
Without any delay
Without hiding
I just want to jump into your white world
And become a warm winter
I want to become a perennial snow lasting thousands of years

—
Moon Chung-hee

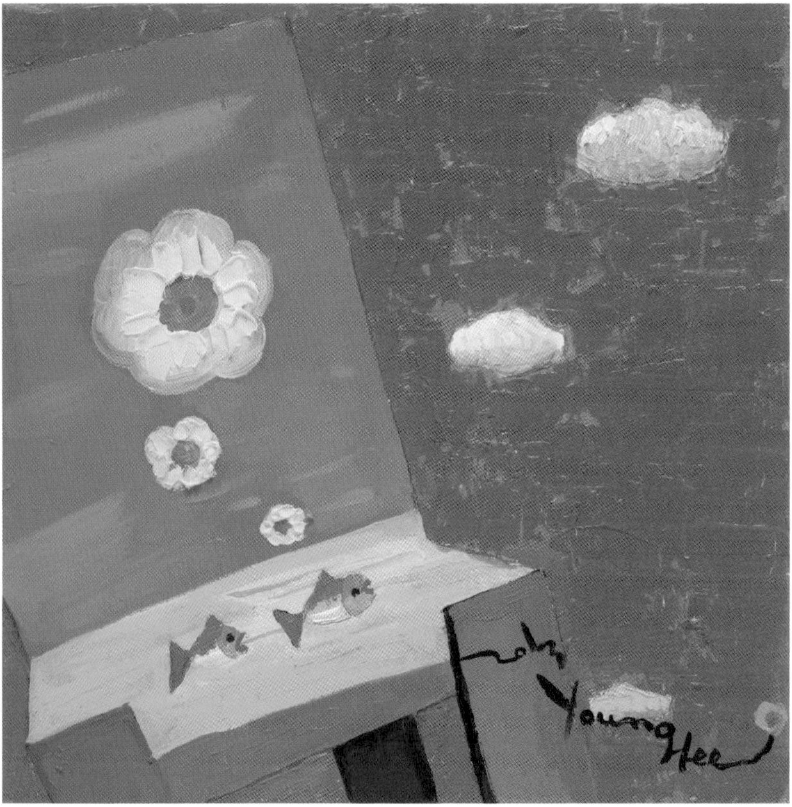
Young Hee

그대에게 가는 길

그댈 만나러 가는 길
나의 맘은 이리도 가볍다
저 하늘의 구름처럼
실려 온 꽃향기처럼

그댈 만나기만 고대한다
마음 가득 설렘이라 한다
나 그댈 품은 채로 봄처럼
곧 너에게 가겠다.

—
이경선

The Way To You

As I make my way to see you
My heart is overflowing with joy
Just like puffs of cloud
Carrying scent of flowers

I eagerly look forward to seeing you
With a fluttering heart
I will soon be there like spring
With full of you within me.

—
Lee Kyungsun

벚꽃 잎

봄의 오후 흩날리는 벚꽃 잎
어떤 마음이기에 이리도 어여쁜가

누군가 품은 사랑의 떨림처럼
내 마음 드리운 그대란 설렘처럼

—
이경선

Cherry Blossom

One spring afternoon, cherry blossoms scatter
What's on its mind to be so beautiful

Like a heart trembling with love
Like thou, the flutter in my heart

—
Lee Kyungsun

2018. Young Hee

산속에서

길을 잃어보지 않은 사람은 모르리라
터덜거리며 걸어간 길 끝에
멀리서 밝혀져오는 불빛의 따뜻함을

막무가내의 어둠속에서
누군가 맞잡을 손이 있다는 것이
인간에 대한 얼마나 새로운 발견인지

산속에서 밤을 맞아본 사람은 알리라
그 산에 갇힌 작은 지붕들이
거대한 산줄기보다
얼마나 큰 힘으로 어깨를 감싸주는지

먼 곳의 불빛은
나그네를 쉬게 하는 것이 아니라
계속 걸어갈 수 있게 해준다는 것을

—
나희덕

In The Mountain

Those who never got lost won't know
The warmth emitted by a distant light
At the end of the road that you've been plodding along

What an incredible discovery about human it is
To find someone's hand that can be held together
In the blunt darkness

Those who encountered night in the mountain will know
How the small rooftops enclosed in the mountain
Can strongly hold your shoulders
More than the vast mountain range

That light from afar
Does not let wayfarer rest
But rather keeps them on the road

—
HeeDuk Ra

서시

단 한 사람의 가슴도
제대로 지피지 못했으면서
무성한 연기만 내고 있는
내 마음의 군불이여
꺼지려면 아직 멀었느냐

—
나희덕

Prelude

A fire in my heart,
Which has yet to properly ignite
Anyone's heart,
Fanning fluffy smoke
Is it far from being extinguished

—
HeeDuk Ra

실수한 후

봄도
처음엔
자꾸만 실수한다

촉촉한 비
훈훈한 바람
꺼내야 하는데
눈발 꺼냈다가
찬바람 꺼냈다가

몇 날 실수하더니
드디어
봄비 뿌리고
봄바람 날린다

푸른 잎사귀
분홍 꽃잎도
꺼내 놓는다

- 잘했어
산과 들이
일어선다

—
박소명

After Stumbling

Spring
Also keeps on stumbling
In the beginning

It is supposed to pull out
Moist drizzle
Pleasant breeze
But instead, it brings out snowflakes and
Cutting winds

Only after jumbling for some time
At last
It sprinkles sun shower and
Softly blows spring breeze

It also unpacks
Green leaves and
Pink petals

- Magnificent
Mountains and valleys are
Awakening

—
Park So Myeong

술에 취한 바다

성산포에서는
남자가 여자보다
여자가 남자보다
바다에 가깝다
나는 내 말만 하고
바다는 제 말만 하며
술은 내가 마시는데
취하긴 바다가 취하고
성산포에서는
바다가 술에
더 약하다

—
이생진

Boozed Ocean

At Seongsan port
Man is closer, more than woman
Woman is closer, more than man
To the ocean
I say what I have to say
Ocean says what it has to say
I drink
But the ocean gets buzzed
At Seongsan port
The ocean is
Weaker to spirits

—
Lee Saengjin

내 마음은

내 마음은 호수요
그대 저어 오오
나는 그대의 흰 그림자를 안고, 옥같이
그대의 뱃전에 부서지리다.

내 마음은 촛불이요
그대 저 문을 닫아 주오
나는 그대의 비단 옷자락에 떨며, 고요히
최후의 한 방울도 남김없이 타오리다.

내 마음은 나그네요
그대 피리를 부러주오
나는 달 아래에 귀를 기우리며, 호젓이
나의 날을 새이오리다.

내 마음은 낙엽이요
잠간 그대의 뜰에 머무르게하오
이제 바람이 일면 나는 또 나그네같이, 외로히
그대를 떠나리다.

—
김동명

My Heart Is

My heart is a lake
Row thou over me
I shall embrace your white shadow
And shatter against your boat like jade.

My heart is a candlelight
Close thou that door for me
I will flutter at your silky fabric,
And silently burn up to the very last drop.

My heart is a wayfarer
Play thou the flute for me
I shall stay up all night under the moonlight,
Alone and be all ears.

My heart is a fallen leaf
Let it linger in your heart briefly
When the wind blows I shall leave you
Like a lonely wayfarer.

—
Kim Dong Myeong

가는 길

그립다
말을 할까
하니 그리워

그냥 갈까
그래도
다시 더 한 번……

저 산에도 까마귀, 들에 까마귀,
서산에는 해 진다고
지저귑니다.

앞 강물, 뒷 강물,
흐르는 물은
어서 따라오라고 따라가자고
흘러도 연달아 흐릅디다려.

—
김소월

On The Way

Thought of saying miss you
Made me
Miss you more

Thought of leaving without saying
But still
Once more……

Crow on that mountain, crow on that field,
Are twittering that
The sun is setting on the west mountain.

Front river, rear river
Flowing river
Urges to follow and be followed
It flows successively even it flows.

—
Kim Sowol

엄마야 누나야

엄마야 누나야 강변 살자,
뜰에는 반짝이는 금모래빛,
뒷문 밖에는 갈잎의 노래
엄마야 누나야 강변 살자.

—
김소월

Mum and Sis

Mum and sis let's live by the riverside,
With the garden full of dazzling golden light,
With songs of reed leaves out of the back door
Mum and sis let's live by the riverside.

—
Kim Sowol

예전엔 미처 몰랐어요

봄 가을 없이 밤마다 돋는 달도
'예전엔 미처 몰랐어요.'

이렇게 사무치게 그리울 줄도
'예전엔 미처 몰랐어요.'

달이 암만 밝아도 쳐다볼 줄을
'예전엔 미처 몰랐어요.'

이제금 저 달이 설움인 줄은
'예전엔 미처 몰랐어요.'

—
김소월

I Didn't Quite Know Before

'I didn't quite know before'
That the moon rises every night regardless of the season.

'I didn't quite know before'
That I would miss you this much.

'I didn't quite know before'
How to look at the moon even when it's brightest.

'I didn't quite know before'
That the moon is the grief.

—
Kim Sowol

돌담에 속삭이는 햇발

돌담에 속삭이는 햇발같이
풀 아래 웃음짓는 샘물같이
내 마음 고요히 고운 봄길 위에
오늘 하루 하늘을 우러르고 싶다.

새악시 볼에 떠오는 부끄럼같이
시의 가슴에 살포시 젖는 물결같이
보드레한 에메랄드 얇게 흐르는
실비단 하늘을 바라보고 싶다.

—
김영랑

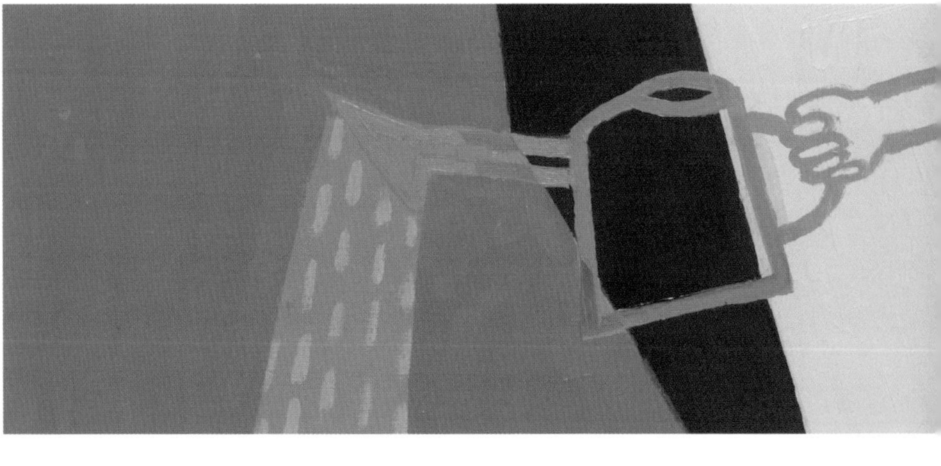

Sunshine Whispering Into The Stonewall

Like a sunshine whispering into the stonewall
Like a spring water smiling below the grass
I want to lay my heart silently on a beautiful spring road
And look up to the sky.

Like a blushing on newly married bride
Like a wave that wets a poet's heart gently
I want to gaze at the silky sky
Where a soft thin layer of emerald flows.

—
Kim Yeongrang

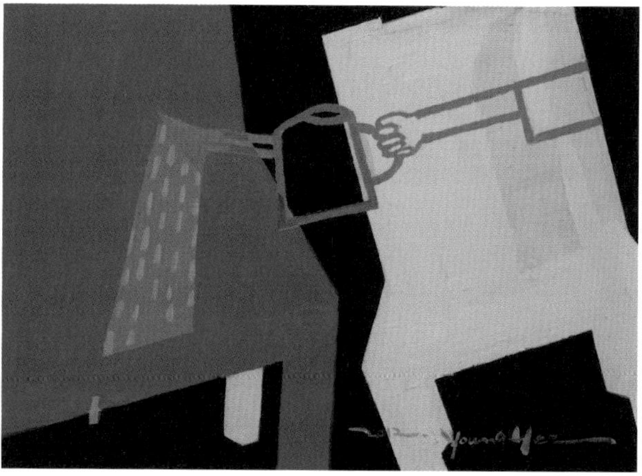

모란이 피기까지는

모란이 피기까지는
나는 아즉 나의 봄을 기둘리고 있을 테요.
모란이 뚝뚝 떨어져 버린 날
나는 비로소 봄을 여읜 서름에 잠길 테요.
오월 어느 날 그 하루 무덥던 날
떨어져 누운 꽃잎마저 시들어버리고는
천지에 모란은 자취도 없어지고
뻗쳐오르던 내 보람 서운케 무너졌느니
모란이 지고 말면 그뿐 내 한해는 다 가고 말아
삼백예순 날 하냥 섭섭해 우옵니다.
모란이 피기까지는
나는 아직 기둘리고 있을 테요.
찬란한 슬픔의 봄을

—
김영랑

Until The Peonies Bloom

Until the peonies bloom
I shall await my spring.
The day when peonies fall apart
I shall dive into sorrow for the loss of spring.
One day in May, the day when it was very hot
Fallen petals wither
Peonies vanish without a trace
My efforts also crumble in dismay
When the peonies wilt, so does my entire year
I cry through 360 days feeling disappointed.
Until the peonies bloom
I shall await.
The spring of glorious sorrow

—
Kim Yeongrang

나그네

강나루 건너서
밀밭 길을

구름에 달 가듯이
가는 나그네

길은 외줄기
남도南道 삼백리

술 익는 마을마다
타는 저녁 놀

구름에 달 가듯이
가는 나그네

—
박목월

Wayfarer

Passing the river dock
Through the wheat field

Wayfarer is walking
Like a cloud drifting across the moon

One way road
120km to the south

Glowing sunset
In every village with fermenting barrels

Wayfarer is walking
Like a cloud drifting across the moon

—
Pak Mok-Wol

기도 1

진흙 빛깔의 얼굴로
땅에 누우면
흙들이 아니라 하고,
그들의 빛깔이 아니라 하고

다시 고개 들어
바로 서면
하늘이 그들과 다르다고
더 멀리 섭니다.

하나님
나는 어디에 서야 합니까
바람이 불어
부는 대로 떠밀리는 낙엽
그들처럼 썩어
쉬일 수 있는 흙은
어디에 있나요

아무도 받아주지 않는
이곳에서
나는 서 있습니다
하늘은 자꾸만 멀어지는데.

—
서정윤

Prayer 1

When lying on the earth
With an earthy hue,
They say I do not belong,
And that my colour is not theirs

When standing up straight
With head raised
The heavens say I am different from them
And they move away.

God the father
Where should I stand
Where is the earth
Where I can decay and mix
Like falling leaves
That sway in the wind

I am standing
Here
Where nobody welcomes
When the heaven is getting further away.

—
Seo Jeongyun

나의 어머니

한 송이 꽃인가 하고 다가서면
한 그루 나무
한 그루 나무인가 하고 다가서면
차라리
한 덩이 바위
한 덩이 바위인가 하고 우러르면
듬직한 산이셨습니다
그러나 어머니는
꽝꽝 언 대지 안에
사랑을 품고 키우는
겨울뿌리
얼음 속에서도 얼지 않는
생명이셨습니다

달빛 받는 외짝 신발처럼
홀로 울음을 가누는
고독한 성자
눈물과 땀과 피
남김없이 흘리시고
그 마지막 죽음까지 뿌리에게 주는
완전한 봉헌이셨습니다

—
신달자

My Mother

When I take a step closer thinking you're a blossom of flower
You were a tree
When I take a step closer thinking you're a tree
You were a rock
When I take a step closer thinking you're a rock
You were a mountain
But my mother
Was winter roots
That holds love
Inside the frozen land
You were a life
That does not freeze in ice cold

Like one lonely shoe under the moonlight
A lonely saint
Holding onto tears
That devotes
Tears, sweat and blood
Without reserve
Even the last death to its roots
You were an absolute dedication

—
Shin dalja

지란지교芝蘭之交를 꿈꾸며

저녁을 먹고 나면 허물없이 찾아가 차 한 잔을 마시고 싶다고 말할 수 있는 친구가 있었으면 좋겠다. 입은 옷을 갈아 입지 않고 김치냄새가 좀 나더라도 흉보지 않을 친구가 우리 집 가까이 살았으면 좋겠다.

비 오는 오후나, 눈 내리는 밤에도 고무신을 끌고 찾아가도 좋을 친구, 밤늦도록 공허한 마음도 마음 놓고 열어 보일 수 있고, 악의없이 남의 얘기를 주고 받고 나서도 말이 날까 걱정되지 않는 친구가… 사람이 자기 아내나 남편, 제 형제나 제 자식하고만 사랑을 나눈다면 어찌 행복해질 수 있을까. 영원이 없을수록 영원을 꿈꾸도록 서로 돕는 진실한 친구가 필요하리라.

그가 여성이어도 좋고 남성이어도 좋다. 나보다 나이가 많아도 좋고 동갑이거나 적어도 좋다. 다만 그의 인품이 맑은 강물처럼 조용하고 은근하며, 깊고 신선하며, 예술과 인생을 소중히 여길 만큼 성숙한 사람이면 된다.

그는 반드시 잘 생길 필요가 없고, 수수하나 멋을 알고 중후한 몸가짐을 할 수 있으면 된다.

때로 약간의 변덕과 신경질을 부려도 그것이 애교로 통할 수 있을 정도면 괜찮고, 나의 변덕과 괜한 흥분에도 적절하게 맞장구쳐주고나서, 얼마의 시간이 흘러 내가 평온해지거든, 부드럽고 세련된 표현으로 충고를 아끼지 않았으면 좋겠다.

Wishing A Noble and Eternal Friendship

I wish I had a friend that I can drop by at ease after a dinner to have a tea. I wish I had a friend nearby who would not mind what I wear even if my clothes smelled like Kimchi.

A friend that I can visit on a rainy afternoon or snowy night in my flip-flops, a friend that I can expose my empty heart till late at night, a friend that I don't have to worry about gossip after conversation… How can one become happy just by sharing love with their spouse, siblings, or children. You would need a true friend who would help one another to dream about eternity as there is no eternity.

That friend can either be a female or male, be older or younger or the same age. As long as the person is tranquil, subtle, deep and clear like a fresh river and is mature enough to cherish art and life.

He does not need to be handsome but be pleasantly simple, elegant and has a dignified demeanour.

Even if he is fickle and tempered at times, it's okay if excused by charm. At times, when I lose my temper, I hope he will go along with me and spare me the advice in delicate and polished words once I become calm after a while.

나는 많은 사람을 사랑하고 싶진 않다. 많은 사람과 사귀기도 원치 않는다. 나의 일생에 한두 사람과 끊어지지 않는 아름답고 향기로운 인연으로 죽기까지 지속되길 바란다. 나는 여러 나라 여러 곳을 여행하면서, 끼니와 잠을 아껴 될수록 많은 것을 구경하였다. 그럼에도 지금은 그 많은 구경 중에 기막힌 감회로 남은 것은 거의 없다. 만약 내가 한두 곳, 한두 가지만 제대로 감상했더라면, 두고두고 되새길 자산이 되었을걸.

우정이라 하면 사람들은 관포지교管鮑之交를 말한다. 그러나 나는 친구를 괴롭히고 싶지 않듯이 나 또한 끝임없는 인내로 베풀기만할 재간이 없다. 나는 도道 닦으며 살기를 바라지 않고, 내 친구도 성현聖賢 같아지기를 바라진 않는다.

나는 될수록 정직하게 살고 싶고, 내 친구도 재미나 위안을 위해서 그저 제자리서 탄로나는 약간의 거짓말을 하는 재치와 위트를 가졌으면 싶을 뿐이다. 나는 때로 맛있는 것을 내가 더 먹고 싶을 테고, 내가 더 예뻐 보이기를 바라겠지만, 금방 그 마음을 지울 줄도 알 것이다. 때로 나는 얼음 풀리는 냇물이나 가을 갈대숲 기러기 울음을 친구보다 더 좋아할 수 있겠으나, 결국은 우정을 제일로 여길 것이다.

우리는 흰눈 속 참대 같은 기상을 지녔으나 들꽃처럼 나약할 수 있고, 아첨 같은 양보는 싫어하지만 이따금 밑지며 사는 아량도 갖기를 바란다.

우리는 명성과 권세, 재력을 중시하지도 부러워하지도 경멸하지도 않을 것이며, 그보다는 자기답게 사는 데 더 매력을 느끼려 애쓸 것이다.

I don't want to be in love with too many people. I do not want to socialize with many people either. I wish that during my lifetime, there will be one or two lovely and fragrant relationships that last till my passing, without any break ups. As I travelled to many different countries and places, I skipped my meals and sleep in order to experience as much as I could. But despite all those excursions, hardly any unforgettable memories remain. If I had thoroughly enjoyed one or two destinations, they would have become lifelong memories that I could cherish for the rest of my life.

When it comes to friendship, the phrase Guan Bao Zhi Jiao[管鮑之交] is frequently used, which alludes to a deep and strong friendship between two people. However, just as I do not want to bother my friends, I do not have the ability to endure and tolerate anything indefinitely. I don't want to live my life while cultivating the Dao, and I don't want my friends to become sages.

As I become older, I simply wish to live my life in all honesty, and I hope my friends have the wit and humour to tell small lies that bring enjoyment and laughs without going too far. Sometimes, I may wish to eat more delicious food and to look more beautiful, but I also know that I can easily dismiss those thoughts. I may appreciate the sound of melting ice in a stream or the cry of migrating geese in an autumn reed field more than my friends at times. But in the end, I will value friendship above all.

We may have the same integrity as the bamboo stump in the snow but still be as fragile as wildflowers, and although we may not be fond of flattering compromise, I hope that we'd be flexible to bear some loss.

We will not admire, covet, or disdain fame, power, or fortune, but rather, we will devote ourselves to cherish our way of living.

우리가 항상 지혜롭진 못하더라도, 자기의 곤란을 벗어나기 위해 비록 진실일지라도 타인을 팔진 않을 것이다. 오해를 받더라도 묵묵할 수 있는 어리석음과 배짱을 지니기를 바란다. 우리의 외모가 아름답진 않다 해도 우리의 향기만은 아름답게 지니리라.

우리는 시기하는 마음 없이 남의 성공을 얘기하며 경쟁하지 않고 자기하고 싶은 일을 하되, 미친 듯이 몰두하게 되기를 바란다.

우리는 우정과 애정을 소중히 여기되 목숨을 거는 만용은 피할 것이다. 그래서 우리의 우정은 애정과도 같으며, 우리의 애정 또한 우정과 같아서 요란한 빛깔도 시끄러운 소리도 피할 것이다.

나는 반닫이를 닦다가 그를 생각할 것이며, 화초에 물을 주다가, 안개 낀 아침 창문을 열다가, 가을 하늘의 흰구름을 바라 보다가, 까닭없이 현기증을 느끼다가, 문득 그가 보고 싶어지며, 그도 그럴 때 나를 찾을 것이다.

그는 때로 울고 싶어지기고 하겠고, 내게도 울 수 있는 눈물과 추억이 있을 것이다.

우리에겐 다시 젊어질 수 있는 추억이 있으나, 늙는 일에 초조하지 않을 웃음도 만들어낼 것이다. 우리는 눈물을 사랑하되 헤프지않게, 가지는 멋보다 풍기는 멋을 사랑하며, 냉면을 먹을 때는 농부처럼 먹을 줄 알며, 스테이크를 자를 때는 여왕보다 품위있게, 군밤을 아이처럼 까먹고, 차를 마실 때는 백작 부인보다 우아해지리라. 우리는 푼돈을 벌기 위해 하기 싫은 일을 하지 않을 것이며, 천 년을 늙어도 항상 가락을 지니는

We may not always be wise but we will not sell others short, despite its truth, just to escape from our predicament. Despite misunderstandings, I hope that we'd be equipped with ignorance and confidence to remain. Let us maintain our fragrance even if our appearance is unappealing.

I hope that we can celebrate each other's successes without jealousy and pursue our goals, yet be immersed in our work without any competition.

We will value our friendship and affection yet avoid temerity of betting our life on it. Thus, our friendship resembles our affection, and our affection is alike to our friendship, so we will avoid any distracting colours and noise.

I will think of him while cleaning the closet, watering the plants, opening misty windows, feeling lightheaded. When I miss him all of a sudden, he too will look for me.

He will grieve from time to time, and I will have tears and memories to cry with him.

We have memories that can make us young again, but we will also create laughter that is unafraid of ageing. We love tears, but not in a sobbing way. We love the elegance that comes from having something, rather than having something itself. We know how to eat cold noodles like a farmer and cut steak more gracefully than a queen. We will eat roasted chestnuts like children, and when we drink tea, we will become more elegant than a noblewoman. We will not do things we dislike only to earn a few pennies. We shall strive to live without losing our free spirit and to be supportive

오동나무처럼, 일생을 춥게 살아도 향기를 팔지 않는 매화처럼, 자유로우 제 모습을 잃지 않고 살고자 애쓰며 서로 격려하리라.

우리는 누구도 미워하지 않으며, 특별히 한두 사람을 사랑한다 하여 많은 사람을 싫어하진 않으리라. 우리가 멋진 글을 못 쓰더라고 쓰는 일을 택한 것에 후회하지 않듯이, 남의 약점도 안쓰럽게 여기리라.

내가 길을 가다가 한 묶음 꽃을 사서 그에게 안겨줘도, 그는 날 주착이라고 나무라지 않으며, 건널목이 아닌 데로 찻길을 건너도 나의 교양을 비웃지 않을 게다. 나 또한 더러 그의 눈에 눈곱이 끼더라도, 이 사이에 고춧가루가 끼었다 해도 그의 숙녀됨이나 그의 신사다움을 의심치 않으며, 오히려 인간적인 유유함을 느끼게 될 게다.

우리의 손이 비록 작고 여리나 서로를 버티어 주는 기둥이 될 것이며, 우리의 눈에 핏발이 서더라도 총기가 사라진 것은 아니며, 눈빛이 흐리고 시력이 어두워질수록 서로를 살펴주는 불빛이 되어 주리라.

그러다가 어느 날이 홀연히 오더라도 축복처럼, 웨딩드레스처럼 수의壽衣를 입게 되리라. 같은 날 또는 다른 날이라도.

세월이 흐르거든 묻힌 자리에서 더 고운 품종의 지란芝蘭이 돋아 피어, 맑고 높은 향기로 다시 만나지리라.

—
유안진

of one another, like a paulownia tree that maintains its posture even after thousand years and a plum flower that retains its scent even in the cold.

We will not hate anyone, and we will not hate others simply because we adore one or two persons. Just as we do not regret choosing to write despite our inability to compose great literature, we will feel sorry for the flaws of others.

Even if I buy him a bunch of flowers while strolling down the street, he won't reject me as being odd, and even if I cross the street somewhere other than a pedestrian crossing, he won't laugh at my manners. I won't doubt her elegance or his gentlemanliness, even if he has gummy eyes or has a piece of red pepper flake between his teeth; instead, I will feel human warmth.

Even though our hands are still small and young, we will become pillars to support one other. Even if our eyes get red with rage, this does not mean that our brilliance has faded. As our vision deteriorates and becomes dark, we will become lights to guide each another.

One day when the day comes with a blessing, we will wear a shroud like a wedding dress. This may or may not be on a same day.

Over time, magnificent orchids will grow where we are buried, and we shall meet again in the form of a gracious and noble fragrance.

—

Yoo Anjin

불행

울고 싶었다.
연약한 풀잎처럼 흐느끼면서
가버린 사람
눈 감는 버릇
그런대로 나의 조그만 불씨같은
격정激情은 더웠다.

언제부턴가
가벼운 미소微笑를 지으며
작별作別의 예의禮儀를 갖추게 된 것은,
의젓하게 손을 잡은 채
나도 한사람 몫의 감정感情을 처리處理한다.

행복幸福도 또한 불행不幸도 아닌
서늘한 초승달밤……
마음이 간절할수록
기도祈禱는 부질없고
텅텅 비어있는 여기 저기에
누구에게나 처럼 벌레는 운다.
행복幸福하고 싶었던 그 시절時節이
실은 행복幸福한 시절時節이었다.
초승 달밤에 이마를 식히며
가버린 사람
눈감는 버릇
쉬 체념諦念하고 안정安定하는 불행不幸
나를 감도는 서늘한 이것은
바람인가,
열도熱度를 잃은 안타까움인가.

—
이형기

Unhappiness

I wanted to cry.
The person that left
While sobbing like a fragile leaf
The habit of closing eyes
My small ember-like passion
Remained as fervent as ever.

For some time
I learned to smile lightly and
Show respect to farewell,
To handle one's share of emotions
While holding hands gracefully.

Neither happy or unhappy
But just a cool crescent moonlit night……
The more desperate one's heart is
The less effective their prayers appear to be and
In the hollow spaces here and there
A bug cries out as to anyone.
Those days that you pursued happiness
In fact, were the days of bliss.
The person who walked away
Cooling their forehead on a crescent moon night
The habit of closing eyes
Unhappiness that gains composure after giving up
Is the chill that hangs in the air
A breeze or,
A melancholy feeling from losing heat.

—
Lee Hyeonggi

산山

작은 산이 큰 산을 가렸으니小山蔽大山
멀고 가까운 곳이 같지 않네遠近地不同

—
정약용

Mountain

A small mountain covers a big mountain
Far and near are not the same

—
Jung Yakyong

호수

얼굴 하나야
손가락 둘로
푹 가리지만,

보고 싶은 마음
호수만하니
눈감을수밖에.

—
정지용

Lake

A face can be
Well covered
By two fingers,

But my longing heart
Is the size of a lake
Thus I can only close my eyes.

—
Chong Chi-Yong

희망

그 별은 아무에게나 보이는 것은 아니다
그 별은 어둠속에서 조용히
자기를 들여다볼 줄 아는 사람의 눈에나 모습을 드러낸다

—
정희성

Hope

That star is not visible to anybody
That star only appears quietly in the dark
To the eyes of those who know how to look into themselves

—
Jung Hee Sung

신년 시新年 詩

흰 구름 뜨고
바람 부는
맑은 겨울 찬 하늘
그 무한을 우러러보며
서 있는
대지의 나무들처럼

오는 새해는
너와 나, 우리에게
그렇게 꿈으로 가득 하여라

한 해가 가고
한 해가 오는
영원한 일월日月의 영원한
이 회전 속에서

너와 나, 우리는
약속된 여로를 동행하는
유한한 생명

오는 새해는
너와 나, 우리에게
그렇게 사랑으로 더욱더
가까이 이어져라.

—
조병화

New Year's Greetings

White cloud
And wind
Against crystal clear winter sky
Like those trees
On earth
Looking up the infinity

Let the New Year
Be full of dreams
To you and I, and us

A year passes
A year comes
Amid this eternal rotation
Of infinite sun and moon

You and I, we
Are finite lives
Travelling through a promised journey

Let the New Year
Bring you and I, and us
Even closer
Together in love.

—
Cho Byung-Hwa

Young Hee

하늘

하늘은 바다
끝없이 넓고 푸른 바다

구름은 조각배

바람이 사공되어
노를 젓는다

—
최계락

The Sky

The sky is the ocean
Infinitely vast blue ocean

Cloud is the boat

Wind becomes
A boatman that rows

—
Choi Kye Rak

님의 침묵

님은 갔습니다. 아아 사랑하는 나의 님은 갔습니다.
푸른 산빛을 깨치고 단풍나무 숲을 향하여 난 작은 길을 걸어서
차마 떨치고 갔습니다.
황금의 꽃같이 굳고 빛나던 옛 맹세는 차디찬 티끌이 되어서
한숨의 미풍에 날아갔습니다.
날카로운 첫 키스의 추억은 나의 운명의 지침을 돌려놓고
뒷걸음쳐서 사라졌습니다.
나는 향기로운 님의 말소리에 귀먹고 꽃다운 님의 얼굴에
눈멀었습니다.
사랑도 사람의 일이라 만날 때에 미리 떠날 것을 염려하고
경계하지 아니한 것은 아니지만 이별은 뜻밖의 일이 되고
놀란 가슴은 새로운 슬픔에 터집니다.
그러나 이별을 쓸데없는 눈물의 원천으로 만들고 마는 것은
스스로 사랑을 깨치는 것인 줄 아는 까닭에 걷잡을 수 없는
슬픔의 힘을 옮겨서 새 희망의 정수박이에 들어부었습니다.
우리는 만날 때에 떠날 것을 염려하는 것과 같이 떠날 때에
다시 만날 것을 믿습니다.
아아 님은 갔지마는 나는 님을 보내지 아니하였습니다.
제 곡조를 못 이기는 사랑의 노래는 님의 침묵을 휩싸고 돕니다.

—
한용운

Silence Of My Beloved

Thou hast left. Ahh, my beloved thou hast left.
Breaking through the blue mountain light, walking on a narrow path towards the maple forest, thou left everything behind.
Rusty vow solid and shining like a golden flower became cold dust and blew away in the breeze of sigh.
Cutting memory of the first kiss transformed my destiny, then disappeared.
I was deafened by your charming voice and I was blinded by your flower-like face.
Love is a human thing, worrying and watching a separation when meeting but surprised heart from unexpected farewell fills with sorrow.
However, I poured this uncontrollable power of sorrow into my head full of hope as I know that making the separation into the source of tears are to comprehend love.
We can't help but think about farewell when we first meet,
At the time of farewell I believe we will meet again.
Ahh, thou hast left but I have not sent you away.
A love song that cannot stand its own melody whirling around your silence.

—

Han Yong-un

사랑하는 까닭

내가 당신을 사랑하는 것은
까닭이 없는 것은 아닙니다
다른 사람들은 나의 홍안만을 사랑하지마는
당신은 나의 백발도 사랑하는 까닭입니다

내가 당신을 기루어하는 것은
까닭이 없는 것이 아닙니다
다른 사람들은 나의 미소만을 사랑하지마는
당신은 나의 눈물도 사랑하는 까닭입니다

내가 당신을 기다리는 것은
까닭이 없는 것이 아닙니다
다른 사람들은 나의 건강만을 사랑하지마는
당신은 나의 죽음도 사랑하는 까닭입니다

—
한용운

Reason For Love

The reason why I love you
Is not without a reason
Others only love my rosy face
But you also love my grey hair

The reason why I yearn for you
Is not without a reason
Others only love my smile
But you also love my tears

The reason why I await for you
Is not without a reason
Others only love my health
But you also love my death

—
Han Yong-un

나의 소망

정결한 마음으로
새해를 맞으리라
그렇게 맞이한 이 해에는
남을 미워하지 않고
하늘같이 신뢰하며
욕심 없이 사랑하리라

소망은 갖는 사람에겐 복이 되고
버리는 사람에겐 화가 오느니
우리 모두 소망 안에서 살아 갈 것이다

지혜로운 사람은
후회로운 삶을 살지 않는다
언제나 남을 섬기는 이치를
배우며 살아간다

선한 도덕과
착한 윤리를 위하여
이해에는 최선을 다하리라

밝음과 맑음을
항상 생활속에 두라
이것을 새해의 지표로 하리라

—
황금찬

My Wish

I shall greet the New Year
With a clear mind
And this New Year
I shall not hate others
But trust like heaven
And love without greed

Hope will be a blessing for those who believes in it
But for those who discards will become temperamental
We shall all live in hope

A wise man
Does not live a regretful life
But lives a life
Learning how to serve others

This New Year
I shall try my best
For morality and ethics

Maintain brightness and clarity
In your life at all times
I shall let this be the New Year's objective

—
Hwang Kum-chan

이렇게 좋은 일이

오민석(문학평론가·
단국대 영미인문학과 교수)

놀라운 일이 벌어졌습니다. 이 부박浮薄한 시대에, 진지한 행위가 조롱의 대상이 되는 시대에 한국의 대표 시들을 모아 그것을 영어로 번역해 알리는 작업을 하겠다는 분들이 나타났습니다. 그들은 문학을 전공한 학자들도 아니고 번역을 전업으로 하는 분들도 아닙니다. 그저 시를 사랑하고, 시를 널리 공유하고 싶고, 번역을 통해 민족 너머의 다수에게 한국 시를 알리고 싶어하는 분들입니다. 그들은 오직 자발적으로, 그 누구의 도움도 없이, 그리고 아무런 대가 없이 이 일에 달려들었습니다. 이 두 분의 이름은 이덕원, 이소정 선생님이십니다.

각기 전문직에 종사하는 이 젊은 부부는 신혼의 '소일거리'로 이 작업을 선택했다고 합니다. 소일거리치고는 이 작업이 얼마나 고상하고 숭고하며 아름답고 힘든 일인지요.

처음 감수를 부탁받았을 때, 저는 한 번도 본 일이 없는 이 부부가 얼마나 고맙고 존경스러웠는지 모릅니다. 이분들은 100여 편의 한국 대표 시들을 자신들의 힘으로 골랐습니다. 한국 시의 유구한 전통과 흐름에 대한 깊은 이해 없이 이런 일은 불가능합니다. 이는 이분들께서 오랜 세월 동안 수많은 한국 시들을 읽어왔고, 즐겨왔으며, 충분히 이해해왔음을 보여줍니다. 이분들은 특정한 관점에 서기보다 보편적이고 대중적인 기준에서 시를 선택했습니다. 이는 가능한 한 많은 사람에게 한국의 대표 시들을 더욱 널리 알리겠다는 의지로 읽힙니다.

How delightful!

Min-Seok, Oh (Literary Critic & Prof. of British and
American Humanities Dpt., Dankook University)

Something amazing has happened. In this mercurial era where sincere actions are often ridiculed, two individuals have emerged who indicated to translate Korea's beloved poems into English and share them widely. They are not scholars who specialize in literature nor are they professional translators. They are individuals that simply love poetry wanting to share and introduce Korean poems to a global audience. They have undertaken this project voluntarily without anyone's urging.

These two individuals are Mr. Dukwon Lee and Mrs. Sojung Lee, a young couple who chose this work as their combined 'hobby' as newlyweds. Considering the nature of this task, it is indeed noble, sublime, beautiful, and challenging at the same time.

When I was first asked to review their work, I cannot describe how grateful I was and how much respect I had for this couple who I have never met before. They selected about 100 poems that represent Korea. This would have been impossible to do so without a deep understanding of the long tradition and history of Korean poetry. This further illustrates that these authors have been reading, understanding, and enjoying countless Korean poems over the years. They chose the poems not from any particular perspective, but from a universal and popular standpoint. This suggests that they have the urge to present Korean poems in the widest manner possible.

그동안 한국의 무수히 아름다운 시들은 단지 주류 언어로 쓰여지지 않았다는 이유만으로 널리 알려지지 않았습니다. 그러나 문학 연구자이자 평론가인 제가 보기에 한국의 시들은 이미 오래전부터 '세계 문학'의 반열을 훌쩍 뛰어넘었습니다. 이제 슬슬 여기저기서 한국의 뛰어난 문학 작품들이 세계 무대에서 선을 보이고 있고, 국가에서도 '한국문학번역원'이란 기구를 통하여 한국문학을 세계에 널리 알리려 하고 있지만, 그간의 문학적 성취에 비해 이 모든 노력은 아직도 부족하기 짝이 없습니다. 이런 와중에 비전문가인 두 분께서 온전히 자신들의 노력으로 그리고 자비로 이런 작업을 한다는 것은 실로 놀라운 일이 아닐 수 없습니다. 그 용기와 패기, 그리고 열정, 그리고 자신의 재능과 자산으로 익명의 수많은 독자들을 섬기는 그 마음을 진심으로 존경하고 사랑합니다.

이 시집의 모든 번역은 무엇보다도 번역자인 두 분의 언어 능력과 감수성의 소산입니다. 감수자의 이름으로 제가 한 것은 이분들이 다 이루어 놓은 것을 그저 한번 훑어본 것뿐이고, 이분들이 다 만들어 놓은 밥상에 눈에 띄지도 않을 작은 찬 하나를 올려놓은 정도입니다. 저는 가능한 한 원본의 의미를 그대로 살리는 쪽으로 감수를 하였습니다. 이덕원, 이소정, 이 젊은 부부의 이 아름다운 작업에 조금이라도 누가 되지 않았기를 빕니다. 그리고 이분들의 번역으로 세계의 수많은 독자에게 널리 소개될 한국의 대표 시들에게도 무궁한 축복이 있기를 간구합니다. 고맙습니다.

Until now, many beautiful Korean poems have not been exposed to the global audience simply because they were not written in a widely spoken language. However, as a literary researcher and a critic, I believe that Korean poetry has long surpassed the ranks of 'world literature'. Korean literature is beginning to get noted on the world stage, and 'Literature Translation Institute of Korea' has been trying to promote Korean literature globally. Despite all these efforts there is still room for improvement. Amid this, it is truly amazing to have these two non-experts working on this project entirely on their own and without any support. I sincerely respect and love their courage, passion, and talent which they are using to serve countless anonymous readers.

All the translations in this poetry collection are the fruit of the two authors' linguistic ability and interpretation. As a reviewer, all I have done is to read over what they have already accomplished and contributed a small dish to the dining table that they have already set. I have made efforts to preserve the original meaning of the poems as much as possible. I hope that my contribution does not dilute this beautiful work of this young couple, Mr. and Mrs. Lee. I hope that these Korean poems, which will be widely introduced to many readers around the world, also receive endless blessings. Thank you.

Young Hee

Wishing From Afar

고대하다 연연하다 성찰하다

옮김 | 이소정, 이덕원
그림 | 이영희

초판 1쇄 발행일 | 2023년 6월 12일
초판 2쇄 발행일 | 2023년 11월 23일

펴낸이 | 신난향
편집위원 | 박영배
펴낸곳 | (주)맥스교육(맥스미디어)
출판등록 | 2011년 8월 17일(제2022-000038호)
주소 | 경기도 성남시 분당구 정자일로156번길 12, 1503호(정자동, 타임브릿지)
전화 | 02-589-5133 팩스 | 02-589-5088
홈페이지 | www.maxedu.co.kr

기획·편집 | 김소연, 김진호
디자인 | 이지안
영업·마케팅 | 이솔기
경영지원 | 장주열

ISBN 979-11-5571-933-6